The
Ravenmaster's
Boy

The Ravenmaster's Boy

MARY HOFFMAN

The Greystones Press

First published in Great Britain in 2017 by

The Greystones Press Ltd
Greystones
37 Lawton Avenue
Carterton
Oxfordshire OX18 3JY

A CIP catalogue record for this book is available
from the British Library

PB 978-1-911122-13-5

1 3 5 7 9 10 8 6 4 2

Designed and typeset by Nigel Hazle

Printe

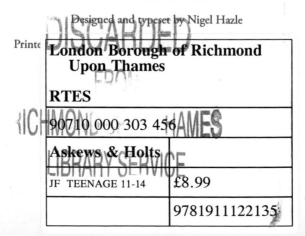

Contents

*For James Lloyd–Mostyn, my son–in–law and
a descendant of Charles Brandon*

PROLOGUE

Back to Life

Kit wasn't the only one who thought he was dead.

The men pushing the cart were making sympathetic noises behind the cloths wrapped round their faces.

'I hate it when there are littl'uns,' one said.

'Yeah, especially ones as young as that. What is she? Six, maybe?'

She! thought Kit. *I'm sorry I never got old enough to get out of these skirts and into my first breeches.*

Then he thought, *But if I can hear them talking, maybe I'm still alive?*

'Carrion for crows now, anyway,' said the first carter.

Unless they are angels, thought Kit.

He knew he was feverish and that nothing was making much sense. He struggled feebly to push away the body that lay on top of him. It was his father – or at least it had been. Kit was trying very hard not to think of it as his father now. It was just a thing, heavy, covered in boils and smelling sickening. Kit retched but the body didn't move.

The body underneath him had been his mother.

Maybe I shall see them in Heaven? thought Kit. He closed his eyes and tried to imagine running into the arms of his warm and laughing mother, or being embraced by his square, strong father.

It took too much effort to forget he was wedged between the smelly and already rotting corpses of the two people he loved best in the world.

So Kit concentrated on imagining freshly baked bread. His parents had been bakers and in happier times the house had been full of that warm and welcoming smell. Heaven would be like that: comforting and clean and full of the promise of food.

Kit hadn't eaten anything for days. Baking – and everything else – had stopped when the plague had entered their house.

I shall be in Heaven soon, he thought. *If I am not dead now I will be very soon. Of plague or of starvation.*

He hoped it would happen before the cart was emptied into the pit and covered with earth. He didn't want to be buried alive.

The Ravenmaster, Thomas Wagstaffe, was walking back to the Tower of London when he spotted the plague-cart, piled high with corpses. He crossed himself and was about to pass over to the other side of the road when something caught his attention.

'Stop!' he said to one of the men pushing the cart. 'I saw a hand move. A child's hand.'

The men were willing enough to stop. Kit felt the weight of his father's body being rolled off him. He dared to open an eye.

'By Our Lady!' said one of the men. 'The maid is alive.'

The Ravenmaster helped them pull the child off the cart.

'Not a mark on her,' said the Ravenmaster. 'Why is she here?'

I'm not a 'she', Kit tried to say but it came out as a feverish mumbling.

'Was in the same house as these two goners,' said the man, scratching his head. 'Parents, we reckoned, and no sign of life in the littl'un.'

'What'll happen to her now?' asked Wagstaffe. A plan was forming in his mind.

The carter shrugged. 'No one left alive near their house and we don't know their names. Just went by the mark on the door. She'll be dead soon enough anyway after being cooped up with her folks and the plague. I wouldn't hold on to her like that.'

'Have you no feelings, man?' said Wagstaffe.

He was holding the small child tenderly. It was not a month since he'd buried his last. Not plague. It was just that his wife Marjorie couldn't seem to hold on to a baby. Either they slipped out early and never breathed or they lasted a few weeks, like their last one, before breathing their last.

This child might go the same way but he felt he had

to try and save her, just as he had done with all his own children.

'I'll take her,' he found himself saying. 'I'll give her a home for however long she lives.'

All Kit knew was that the bad smell had faded and he was being held in strong arms.

It was good that he didn't try to speak again. The Ravenmaster carried him hidden under his cloak up to the gate of the Tower, while the cart trundled on its way to the dreadful pit.

'What you got there, Tom?' asked the warder on the gate.

'Meat for the birds,' he answered. And it was true. Under his other arm he had a package from the butcher and it was awkward getting through the postern gate with two such bundles.

His wife was sitting in their room with her hands in her lap. She was still weak from the birth of their last baby and it had taken longer than usual for her milk to dry up. His heart hurt to see her so thin and defeated.

He threw back his cloak and Marjorie gasped to see the pathetic bundle.

'Who is that? Where did you find her?'

The Ravenmaster very much did not want to tell his wife that he had pulled this half-dead child off a plague cart and that she would probably not live long. But they did not have secrets from each other, so in the end he told her exactly what had happened.

'Come here, pet,' she said and took the child, chafing its cold hands. The bundle opened its brown eyes.

'What's your name, little one?' asked Marjorie.

'Christopher,' croaked the child. 'Called Kit. Are you an angel?'

'By Saint Peter!' said the Ravenmaster. 'I swore it was a girl.'

Their little Mary was the last child they had buried. It was a girl he thought his wife would cherish. But he had underestimated his wife's maternal instincts.

'Not an angel, love,' said Marjorie. 'Just a woman. But let's get some food into you and warm you up.'

As Kit felt her arms around him he wasn't at all sure that he hadn't gone to Heaven.

1

A New Queen for an Old King

NINE YEARS LATER

'More blood?' asked Bran hopefully.

'Not today,' said Kit. 'Don't be greedy.'

Only Kit Wagstaffe, the Ravenmaster's boy, could get away with addressing the biggest of the ravens like that. But then only Kit could speak fluent Raven.

It had begun not long after he got his first breeches and his new father took him to meet the big black birds.

Bran had shed a tail feather, long and glossy, and Kit picked it up from the grass on Tower Green. Something about its perfection struck him as magical: it seemed wrong either to leave it on the ground or take it for himself.

He knelt and proffered it back to the bird like a knight offering his sword to a king.

But what happened next was beyond human understanding.

'That big old bird took the feather in his beak and brushed Kit's mouth with the plume,' the Ravenmaster told his wife. 'And then he did the same on both his ears! Then he dropped it at Kit's feet and they both bowed. I've never seen anything like it.'

And from that day, Kit and the ravens understood one another perfectly.

Kit had almost forgotten his other life; it felt as if he had always lived within the thick honey-coloured walls of the Tower of London. He knew that Thomas and Marjorie weren't really his parents but he could no longer remember the faces of his first mother and father and had been content to take the Ravenmaster's name.

As for the Wagstaffes, they might have got their son when he was nearly seven but he was to them all they had ever wanted in a child. He grew and thrived and learned his letters and was as loving as any natural son could have been. And to them he was a miracle: not just a son but a child who had survived the plague. And one who could speak with ravens.

The only time Kit remembered his first life was when the smell of fresh loaves reached him from the bakery in the palace and he would drift over to talk to Isabel, the baker's daughter.

Now, at sixteen he had become the Ravenmaster's apprentice and was highly likely to succeed him in the job. No one else had ever had such an understanding with the birds.

'No more blood?' asked Bran. 'Bread dipped in blood?'

'Not today,' said Kit firmly. 'You've had all you're getting. But maybe there will be a hen's egg for you later.'

Bran preened his wing feathers.

'All well, lad?' asked the Ravenmaster.

They had finished cleaning out the cages the ravens used at night.

'Bran wants more bread soaked in blood,' said Kit.

He was used to acting as interpreter between his father and the birds. The older ravens sometimes said words like 'Good morning' that all could understand but no one had conversations with them the way Kit did. And only Kit knew that Bran was the King Raven.

'There'll be blood enough to satisfy even old Bran soon,' said the Ravenmaster. He looked grim, as he often did these days. Then he shook his head.

'Take no notice of me, son,' he said. 'Things haven't been right ever since they took those two old men out to the hill and lopped their heads off.'

Kit looked round uneasily. Even at his age he knew there were things it wasn't wise to talk about when others might be listening.

He remembered the two old men last summer: John Fisher and Thomas More. They had been prisoners in the Tower for months but his father hadn't been able to explain properly why. Something to do with the new queen.

They were kept in the Bell Tower, one on top of the other, the older one in the upper room and the younger on the ground floor.

The ground floor prisoner was called Thomas, like Kit's father, and had once been a great man and chancellor of England. He walked in the gardens every day and had often given Kit a nod of greeting on his way to Mass in the chapel.

The other one was even grander – he was made a cardinal soon after being imprisoned in the Tower, but Kit's father said it was bad news, that the king was against all cardinals now, even against the Pope, so it would do old Bishop John no good to be given a scarlet hat.

'The king said he'd send Fisher's head to Rome, sooner than have his new hat sent here.'

Kit hadn't understood that; there was no sign of any red hats in the Bell Tower, only pious old men saying their prayers. Perhaps the king had stopped the hat arriving? But Kit couldn't see what would have made him so angry about a hat.

Anyway, it wasn't long before old Fisher had no need of any hat. Kit couldn't see how the two men could be traitors to the king. They seemed so harmless and dignified. But one after the other last summer, with less than three weeks between them, they were taken out of their prison cells and off to Tower Hill, where their heads had been chopped off.

Kit had not been allowed to go, though his father

had been on duty in the crowd that gathered to see both executions. Since then he had often been gloomy and grim, like this morning.

But Kit had seen the heads. First Fisher's was put on a spike on London Bridge but once the other old man had been killed, the first head was tossed down into the river and Thomas More's put in its place. People said that these grisly relics had to be displayed to stop others committing treason but Kit always shuddered and hurried past quickly if he had to cross the bridge.

It was a bitterly cold January day and, when the birds were done, father and son walked over to the bakery to warm their hands and stomachs with a new-baked loaf.

Isabel was up early as always, helping her father.

'Good morrow, Ravenmaster,' she said, dropping Kit's father a quick curtsey. All the Tower workers showed respect to the warders; it made Kit feel proud of his father, even though Isabel showed little respect to a boy like him.

She was very flushed this morning and not just from the heat of the ovens.

'Have you heard the news?' she whispered to Kit.

He warmed his numb fingers on the small hot loaf. But before Isabel could impart her news, they heard the baker telling it to the Ravenmaster.

'The queen is dead?' said Kit, nearly dropping the bread.

'Shh! Not "the queen". We aren't allowed to call her that. The "dowager princess" is what you have to say if you want to keep your head on your shoulders.'

'But the one who used to be called Queen Katherine?' asked Kit. He wanted to be sure to get it right. 'The king's first wife?'

'Not according to the king,' whispered his friend. 'But yes, the one who *was* old Queen Katherine. She's dead.'

'So there really is only one queen now,' said Kit.

'You are so slow sometimes, Kit Wagstaffe,' said Isabel. 'It makes me long to box your ears! Yes of course there is only one queen. How could there be two? Don't you remember Queen Anne's coronation?'

Kit thought he would never forget it; it had been the best day of his life. The guns all firing and the barges covered in gold leaf and tinkling with bells! Heralds and minstrels all playing and the beautiful young queen with her black hair loose down her back.

There weren't many young ones living in the Tower and even Isabel was a year older than him and well on the way to being a woman. She often scolded him these days and didn't play as many games as she had when they were younger.

Then there was Alice, the lieutenant's daughter, who was Kit's age and so beautiful that she seemed to Kit far above the likes of him and the few children of Yeoman Warders. But all the young ones – and they had been three years younger then – had been allowed to watch the queen's procession as the barges came up the river from Greenwich.

Kit's father, who had been part of the welcoming party, told them how Queen Anne had been greeted by the king:

'He put his hands on either side of her face and kissed her right heartily,' he said. 'No doubt but the king and queen are much in love.'

'Ay, and she six months gone with his baby,' said Marjorie, who had lost so many of her own.

But there had been something in the room that Kit couldn't quite identify – some feeling that his parents were not completely happy about the way things were.

Kit and his father walked back across the green, the grassy area where the ravens spent a lot of their time. Thomas had told Kit that once a man had been beheaded there, on the orders of King Richard the Third. It made Kit shiver to think of someone's life oozing out along with the blood from his neck. It must hurt such a lot. He was glad that the two old men last summer had lost their lives outside the Tower walls.

'We will go and say a prayer in the chapel for the old queen's soul,' said his father. 'And then we will never speak of her again.'

There were five ravens at the Tower for Kit to talk to. Bran was the king of them but had no queen since his mate had died the year before. Then there were two pairs: Huginn and Muninn, known as Hugh and Moony –

only Kit knew their real names. The younger pair were Thomas and Bess, named for the king's secretary and Henry's little daughter by Queen Anne.

Although Kit could talk to them all, he knew that Thomas and Bess were just ordinary birds, even though he found nothing ordinary about ravens. The other three had special qualities.

He was talking to them and feeding them their disgusting bloody pieces of meat three days later when there was a sudden startling sound of heralds' trumpets from the main gate. Kit's parents came rushing out towards the green, Marjorie drying her hands on her apron.

'What is it?' asked Kit. The ravens seemed agitated.

'That, my lad,' said the Ravenmaster, 'is the sound of a royal visit.'

'And you with crumbs in your beard,' scolded his wife.

'Well, they aren't very likely to come here,' he said, brushing off Marjorie's attempts to smarten him up.

'They are,' Bran croaked to Kit. 'The king is coming to see me.'

'Bran says the king is visiting him,' Kit translated.

'That bird has ideas above his station,' said the Ravenmaster. But he was used to Kit's superior understanding of the birds and straightened his tunic all the same.

And 'that bird' was right. The sound of trumpets and minstrels was getting nearer. Soon they could see the constable of the Tower, Sir William Kingston, leading a great party of well-dressed courtiers towards the green.

'Too much bright finery so soon after the old queen's death,' grumbled the Ravenmaster. 'They're wearing yellow!'

'Shh!' hissed his wife furiously. 'Do you want to be dragged out on Tower Hill and your foolish head taken off you for a traitor? If the king comes here you are to say nothing about Queen Katherine!'

Kit was alarmed, because the king's party definitely *was* heading for the green. And because his father had already broken his resolution to speak no more about old Queen Katherine. Bran started to preen his tail feathers. He looked comically like Kit's father brushing crumbs from his beard.

'There's a raven with them!' said Kit.

And there was: one of the king's attendants carried a tethered and hooded raven on his arm. The Tower ravens were all excited to see another of their kind and flapped and cawed till Bran silenced them with a look.

As the party approached, Marjorie whipped off her apron and curtseyed low to the ground, somehow managing to dig both her son and husband with her elbows at the same time, to force them into a respectful bow.

'Ah, Ravenmaster!' said the king. 'I am pleased to find you here. We have brought you a new recruit.'

Kit heard the rich sonorous voice rolling out around

the green but could see nothing of his monarch but his legs in white silk stockings and boots. He was petrified; he had never met the king before. And beside the king's fine leather boots was a small pair of figured velvet slippers.

Fancy wearing such flimsy shoes outdoors in January, thought Kit. He dared to raise his eyes.

And there was the queen! She was little, not as tall as sixteen-year-old Kit, her long black hair coiled up in a coif this morning. And so beautiful! She smiled at Kit and he felt himself blushing like a fool.

Meanwhile King Henry had motioned the man with the raven forwards and Kit saw his father take the handsome black bird from him and bow again to the king.

'Thank you, Your Majesty,' said the Ravenmaster. 'How very kind.'

'It is a female, I'm assured by the Welsh lord who gave it to me,' the king was saying.

'That is most welcome, sire, since our oldest bird has lost his mate.'

Bran was staring hard at the new bird. He raised his head feathers.

'She is called Blodwen, I believe,' said the king.

Then he seemed to lose interest in the ravens and their master and turned to the constable.

'We shall take refreshment with you now, Kingston.'

The party moved off and were gone as quickly as they came, like a vision of Fair Folk in a dream.

'Did that really happen?' asked Kit. 'The king came and talked to you?'

'Well, here is Blodwen to prove it,' said his father. He talked soothingly to the bird.

'Another mouth to feed,' said Marjorie, not unkindly. She was still shaking from the shock of the royal visit and tied her apron tightly back round her middle to settle herself.

Kit realised he was still clutching a strip of meat and had been all the time he was bowing to the queen. He held it out to the new arrival, who took it in her beak and swallowed.

'She's a beauty,' he told Bran in Raven.

'So elegant and delicate,' said Bran admiringly.

'Well, I'd better keep her in a cage till she gets used to us,' said the Ravenmaster. He settled Blodwen, who had not yet said anything, on a perch in one of the big raven cages and fastened it shut. Bran immediately flew into the cage beside hers and started to make soft welcoming noises through the bars.

'Look how pleased old Bran is to have a new mate,' said Thomas. 'He's like the king. Thinks it's easy enough to get a new young queen when the old one dies or doesn't suit any more.'

'Qu'aark!' cawed Bran.

'You've offended him,' said Kit. 'He was really fond of his old wife and sad when she died.'

'Yes, he's worn black ever since as a mark of respect,' said Marjorie. 'Come along the pair of you. Stop treating

16

those birds like people and get yourselves spruced up and down to the gate. You must be there to make reverence to the king and queen when they leave or they'll think you're ungrateful.'

2

'The King is Dead'

One of the first books Kit had learned to read from, soon
after he came to live in the Tower, was the Ravenmaster's
most treasured posession. At first when Thomas pulled
the heavy, leather-bound book out of a chest, Kit's heart
had sunk. Stamped on the cover in big gold letters were
the words:

LIBER CORVIDARUM

He had no idea what they meant.

'I don't know any Latin besides my prayers,' he told
his father.

'No more do I, son,' said Thomas. 'But see here,
inside. It has been done into English.'

There were handwritten pages interleaved between
the dense printed ones and these Kit could just about
make out on his own.

'It was a Ravenmaster of nearly a hundred years ago
that wrote the *Book of Ravens*,' said Thomas. 'And another

one – the one before me – who wrote it all out again in English so that you don't have to be a scholar to read it.'

'The *Book of Ravens*,' read Kit.

The English version was by Robert Comynes, Ravenmaster of the Tower of London, made in the year 1525, not long before Kit had come to live in the Tower.

'What happened to Comynes?' Kit asked.

'Died,' said Thomas. 'The year after he finished the book. His life's work was done. I was his apprentice and the constable asked me to take over.'

'Can I read it?'

'I want you to. If you study it hard, you'll know as much about the birds as I do. Though there's no susbstitute for getting acquainted with the real ones.'

Kit thought of the big black beaks, the glossy feathers and the bright intelligent eyes and nodded. He would make that book his Bible. Not that he could read the real Bible, which was all in Latin. Some of it had been translated into English but that was for some reason frowned on and there were no English pages stuck into the Bible used in the Tower chapel, as far as Kit could tell.

And now that the king had brought them a new mate for Bran, Kit took out the old book and re-read everything he could find about pairs of ravens.

The birds mate for life, he read, *and if one of a pair dies the other seems to mourn just like a man for his wife. But after some space of time, a new bird may be introduced, just as a man may find himself a new wife.*

Kit thought of the king and his new queen. He had liked what he saw of her, with her sparkling black eyes and her bold smile. He had never seen the old queen, who had been packed off to Huntingdonshire because, so people said, the king had tired of her because she hadn't given him a son and was besides getting old and fat.

Kit didn't remember who had told him all this but there was something about it that unsettled him. He shrugged it off. The old queen was dead now anyway, the king had his new mate and, though pretty Queen Anne hadn't had a son yet, she surely would do. And there was the little princess that Bess the raven was named after. Surely the king would have a whole clutch of young ones before long. And maybe Bran would too.

Bran was enchanted by Blodwen. Within a few days, the Ravenmaster opened her cage and Bran flew in, settling on the perch beside her and raising his head feathers, inviting her to groom him. The female cautiously responded, preening Bran's feathers and letting him do the same to her.

Kit tried not to eavesdrop on what they were saying to each other. But he smiled to himself.

He went to see if Isabel was busy; he hadn't seen her since the king's visit.

'Did you see the queen?' he asked her, when they'd chatted for a while. He knew Isabel would be bound to have an opinion.

She looked round to check they weren't being

overheard before she answered. Kit had noticed a lot of people doing that lately.

'She's a bold one, isn't she?' said Isabel. 'Flaunting her victory so in her yellow dress.'

'Was she?'

'Oh yes. Her old rival dead and a new baby under her bodice.'

'A new baby?'

'Couldn't you tell? Of course not – boys never can. I'd say she was about four months gone.'

Kit blushed; how *did* girls know this sort of thing? Isabel hadn't had any more babies than he'd had himself and yet she seemed so sure.

'So the king might soon have the son he wants?'

'Let's hope so – for the queen's sake,' said Isabel, again with that cautious quick glance round.

'Well, I liked her,' said Kit. 'I thought she was a fine lady.'

But to that he got no more than a contemptuous snort from his friend.

Kit hoped he might see the queen again when his father took him to Greenwich Palace just over a week later to see the tournament. The king loved these entertainments. King Henry had a mighty reputation in the lists and had loved to joust ever since he was a boy. The only knight ever to match him was Charles Brandon, Duke of Suffolk, who was careful always to let his boyhood friend win at the last.

The queen was there, watching from the royal pavilion as King Henry put on his armour.

'Isabel says Queen Anne's having another baby,' Kit told his father, trying to see if she looked any plumper than her waiting women.

But nothing could distract him for long from the colour and excitement of a full-blooded tournament. He would have loved to get dressed in a suit of armour and ride a big war horse but it was a sport too expensive for anyone except the nobility. Still, the next best thing was to watch as two knights in full armour, with their destriers wearing their colours, charged at each other with lowered lances.

There was not just jousting in the lists: there were melées, when two lines of nobles on horseback charged together and fought in a wonderful mass until the last man was left standing. And tilting at the quintain, where a single knight charged at a target, which could swing round and knock him off his horse. That was quite fun to watch, especially when the knight didn't get out of the way quickly enough.

But today the jousting was interrupted before it had properly begun.

The king was practising on his great horse by running at a ring with his lance.

It was easy to pick out King Henry from the rest of the nobles, with his vivid colours of red, blue and gold, and he rode so fast that the colours all mixed together in a blur of lions and lilies as he hurtled towards the ring, his lance outstretched. Kit found he was standing and screaming encouragement – and so was everyone else, in hope that the king would joust today.

And then something horrible happened.

The king's warhorse stumbled and fell and Henry was on the ground with the full weight of the horse on top of him, both fully armoured. The crowd cried out with one voice in horror. The king lay very still.

'Is he dead?' Kit asked, not daring to look.

'I don't know,' said the Ravenmaster. 'Look, men are lifting him.'

Many servants ran into the lists and pushed and pulled at the horse, whose own heavy armour was preventing him from getting to his feet. Miraculously, he struggled up and walked away unharmed. Squires ran to take the horse's armour off. Kit kept watching but the huge figure on the ground lay very still.

More servants fetched a hurdle and moved the king very gently on to it. A nobleman removed the king's helmet.

'That's the Duke of Suffolk,' said Thomas. 'He nearly killed the king in another joust twelve years ago.'

'So the king's had accidents before and survived?'

'Yes, and that was a bad one. The king's visor was up and the duke's lance caught him in the face. With luck, this time he's just badly winded.'

But Kit thought that a destrier in full armour might do more damage landing on top of you than just knock the breath out of you. That horse could have broken every bone in the king's body.

But he wasn't to find out for a while.

'Come on, Kit,' said his father. 'We'd better be getting back to the Tower. The king will need every man at his post. That's the best way to help him.'

There was nothing to be done but get on with their work. The ravens were unusually noisy, making alarm calls that sounded so human that Thomas looked up, startled, every time.

'Ask them what's the matter, Kit,' he said. 'It's making me nervous.'

Kit went to Bran, who was perching next to Blodwen. She seemed anxious and Bran was making comforting noises, little murmurs and whispers, like the calls the birds made when roosting for the night.

'Good evening, Your Majesty,' he said. 'Can you tell me what's upsetting all the ravens?'

'There's a rumour on the air,' said Bran. 'Birds all over London are saying the king is dead.'

It was a cold day but Kit suddenly felt much colder.

'I saw him fall, at the tournament,' he told the old bird. 'His horse fell on top of him. He didn't move.'

'It is too soon to mourn him yet,' said Bran. 'A rumour is all it is. The birds have been known to be wrong.'

Kit thought about the queen and her little daughter, Elizabeth, and how awful it would be for them if the king were really dead. Would Elizabeth be queen? Surely she was too small?

He went to tell his father what the birds were saying.

It was a quiet evening in Kit's home. After all the tensions of last year, when the two old men had been killed, it had seemed that things were settling down. The old queen was dead, the new queen might be pregnant, the king was happy. And then – out of the blue – everything was in chaos again.

It wasn't until late next morning that they heard the news. The king was alive; the king would live.

As the days wore on, it was clear that it had been a close thing. Henry had been unconscious for two hours and his doctors had been very grave.

As usual, it was Isabel who gave Kit the most important news: a few days after the king's accident – the very day of old Queen Katherine's funeral – the queen had miscarried a child.

'And they say it was boy,' she whispered to him, giving him a flaky almond pastry to sweeten the tale.

'But that's awful!' said Kit.

'The Duke of Norfolk told her how badly the king was hurt at the tournament and the fright started the baby coming.'

'And it was too soon?'

'Far too soon. The baby was less than four months grown. Some are saying it's the old queen's revenge – to reach out from her grave and snatch her usurper's baby.'

Kit took a large bite of his pastry and thought of his second mother, Marjorie, who had lost so many babies before her time. It didn't seem right that nothing could save the queen – the highest lady in the land – from sharing the fate of an ordinary woman. No medicine or doctors that could help, when she could afford the best the country had to offer.

'And,' Isabel said even more softly, 'they say the king is disgusted with her and told her he would make no more babies with her if she couldn't give him the son he needs.'

Kit swallowed a bite of pastry, which felt dry in his throat. 'How do you *know* all this?'

He thought that he was kept well informed by Bran and the other birds but they hadn't told him any of this detail.

'Women just hear these things and pass them on,' said Isabel. 'Great people think they have their secrets but they never suppose that their servants overhear everything. They don't realise common people have ears and minds.'

Was it true? Kit could picture the scene: the beautiful queen in bed and probably weeping for the loss of her child, the king angry and disappointed, the Duke of Norfolk feeling guilty that he hadn't been more gentle in telling the queen of the seriousness of her husband's fall. Or maybe it had been the shock of seeing it happen that had shaken the baby out of the queen's body. Kit didn't know if that was possible.

Would it have made any difference if the duke had been gentler? Or if it hadn't been the day the old queen went into the earth?

'Hey, Bird Boy!' said a harsh voice behind him. It

was George Atwood, whose father was keeper of the lions and leopards. Kit usually kept out of George's way. Now he just nodded, his mouth full of sugar and nuts.

'Stuffing your face, as usual,' said George. 'How about a pastry for me, Isabel? Or do you keep all your favours for the boy that cleans the bird cages?'

'You may have a pastry if you pay me a farthing as Kit did,' lied Isabel smoothly. 'If your hands are clean. I imagine that lions make a much worse mess than a few birds.'

George paid his money meekly; Isabel was his weak spot. Kit was pleased to see that she was no more gracious to George than to him, though he knew she really was a good friend. Atwood tended to give himself airs because his father looked after the menagerie.

'Want to come and see our new bear?' he asked Isabel.

'I don't have to come to the menagerie to see bears,' she said. 'Most of my customers are like that till they are fed.'

'Ah, but he's a big one,' said George. 'And as bad-tempered as the king.'

All three of them looked round guiltily, even George.

'I'd be bad-tempered if you set mastiffs on me,' said Isabel, who hated the bear-baiting shows held for visitors.

'Don't be such a girl,' said George. 'It's good sport.'

'Not for the bear with the bloody muzzle or the dogs

thrown so hard their backs are broken,' said Isabel. 'Now take your pastry and go. I have baking to help with.'

The two boys left her and walked back towards the Lion Gate where the wild animals were held captive. Kit didn't particularly want to see the bear or spend time with George Atwood. His head was still full of what Isabel had told him about the queen and her lost baby. So much so that he didn't notice that George had stopped walking and Kit cannoned into him. George was bowing and Kit nearly knocked him over.

He heard a familiar musical laugh and there was Alice Walsingham coming towards them with her father the lieutenant. Kit managed a hasty bow while George scrambled back into a respectful position.

'Hello, boys,' said the lieutenant. 'On your way to see the bear? Alice and I have just paid him a visit.'

Then he stopped and frowned.

'I have just remembered something. Would you please escort Alice back to my lodgings? I need to attend court.'

The boys fell over themselves to offer Alice their arms and she cheerfully took both of them.

'Will you be all right, Alice?' her father asked. 'I'm not sure the bear wouldn't be a less clumsy attendant.'

'I will be perfectly all right, Father,' said Alice, smiling and dimpling most delightfully, Kit thought. 'Indeed, I think I could manage to find my way back home even without Kit and George to accompany me. It's only a few yards!'

The lieutenant raised his hat to them and the three children of the Tower walked back over the cobbles to the part of the Tower where Alice lived with her father, her brother and two sisters. She had lost her mother at an even earlier age than Kit had and had once told him she couldn't remember her.

'How are the ravens?' she asked Kit. 'You are so brave to work with them, with their huge beaks and claws.'

George cleared his throat importantly. 'They are nothing to lions and leopards though! They couldn't kill you.'

Kit wasn't so sure about that, but he let George carry on boasting about how dangerous his father's animals were. He was content, on this fine winter day, just to walk alongside pretty Alice for a few minutes. They were soon at the lieutenant's lodgings and Alice thanked them both equally before going in.

'I know what you're thinking,' said George, 'and you had better stop thinking it. Alice is not for you.'

Kit blushed. 'I don't know what you mean.'

'Yes you do, but I'm telling you – my father is of much higher estate than yours. He's a king's man, like the lieutenant. Not a common warder.'

Kit wondered what George would say if he'd known Kit's first father had been a baker.

'What has that got to do with anything?' he asked.

'Alice will marry a nobleman – a knight at least,' said George, not realising the trap he was walking into.

'Oh, like you?' said Kit. 'I'm sorry, Sir George.

I hadn't realised you had been dubbed by the king's sword.'

George lunged at him and Kit had time only to think how good it had felt to provoke his enemy, before they were both rolling on the ground, punching and kicking, and he remembered how much bigger than him George was.

3

Prisoners

It took weeks for Kit's bruises to fade but there was no permanent harm done. Marjorie scolded him for fighting and the Ravenmaster would have beaten him but relented when he saw the ugly marks the cobbles had made on Kit's back as the heavier George had rolled on top of him and pummelled him into the ground.

Isabel was unsympathetic.

'George is a clod,' she said. 'But what were you arguing about? It was madness to provoke him.'

'I like that!' objected Kit. 'How do you know he wasn't the one doing the provoking?'

But he didn't say they had been fighting about Alice. Kit kept well away from the lieutenant's quarters until his face had healed.

He spent more and more time with the ravens. Bran's romantic life was going better than Kit's – Blodwen had accepted the older bird as her mate. They were now inseparable. But, beautiful and glossy as she was, Kit knew that Blodwen was an ordinary raven, like Thomas and Bess, not a magical one like the other three.

Bran had been more sympathetic than Isabel.

'Nasty fight that must have been,' he croaked. 'Would you like me to find your foe and bite him?'

Kit shook his head; he feared what might happen to any bird that attacked George and he didn't want King Bran to end up as lion food.

He took the big bird carefully in his arms. 'Time to trim your flight feathers, Your Majesty,' he said.

Bran never minded having his feathers clipped in this way – none of the birds did. They had plentiful food at the Tower and they could fly enough to give them exercise. They didn't want to escape.

'I want Blodwen to see that it doesn't hurt you,' said Kit. 'You must explain that she has to have hers done too.'

Carefully, he trimmed just enough from Bran's feathers to keep him from flying outside the confines of the Tower walls. This had been Kit's job for a long time now. The birds would let his father do it but since the Ravenmaster didn't speak Raven, they couldn't always understand his words of reassurance. Kit's father had received many a nasty bite, even though the birds always held back and didn't do as much damage as they were capable of.

Kit hoped the king might visit again, now he had recovered from his fall in the tournament. He found himself thinking about the queen a lot. She had seemed so lively that it was hard to imagine her tired and ill and upset about her lost baby. Kit wondered if she would have spent time with the little princess to comfort herself. Kit's father had seen Princess Elizabeth once, he said: a chattering little thing with red-gold curls, being carried by her proud father. It was a shame she hadn't been born a boy.

'They were so sure it would be a prince that there was hardly room to change the word to "princess" on the Royal Proclamation,' his father said. 'And they cancelled the tournament planned to celebrate the prince's birth.'

But the king and queen didn't come again and gradually, mainly through Isabel and her endless store of gossip, it began to seem as if all was not well at the palace. A cold, harsh winter was giving way to the coming of spring but not in King Henry's heart.

'They say the king is tired of his new queen,' Isabel told him, 'and might be looking for another.'

Kit couldn't understand it. 'But he went to such trouble to get rid of the old queen and get this new one,' he whispered, still careful because you weren't supposed to call the dead Katherine 'queen'.

Isabel shrugged. 'It would probably all be well still if she had given him the son he needs but now he has said he will have no more babies with her. And he needs a boy to be the next king, so I think there will be a new queen before long.'

Kit went to the ravens to talk about it.

'We shall ask for news from the birds,' said Huginn.

Kit noticed that the ravens never referred to themselves as 'birds'. It was as if they were a race apart.

'Royal personages never notice a sparrow or a robin pecking at something on their windowsills,' said Muninn.

'And can all birds understand when humans speak?' asked Kit.

'We can,' said Thomas. 'But it's a rare human who can understand us.' If ravens could smile, Kit understood that Thomas would have smiled at him now.

'Pigeons are especially good at remembering what they have heard,' said Bran. 'The little kinds are sometimes a bit bird-brained. I shall send a pigeon to listen at the secretary's window. That's where all the news comes from these days.'

The king's secretary was called Thomas Cromwell; he was the one that Thomas the raven was named for. Though the man hadn't been secretary then, only a sort of adviser to the king. Kit had seen him several times when Cromwell had been supervising some repairs at the Tower. He was a stocky fellow with a grim, determined face, but everyone said he was the cleverest man in England.

And after a few weeks, Bran's army of pigeon spies brought interesting news. Cromwell had quarrelled with the queen.

'That was very foolish of her, whatever it was about,' said Marjorie when Kit told her. She had quite got used to the way her son collected information from the birds. 'If she has both the secretary and the king against her, as Isabel told you, then she is in a very dangerous situation.'

'You seem sorry for her, Mother,' said Kit. 'I thought you didn't like her.'

'I don't,' said Marjorie. 'At least I don't like what she did, leading the king away from his true wife. But it's treason to say that or even think it, so don't go repeating it outside these walls. Some might say Anne deserves whatever punishment is coming her way. But if the king decided to divorce her and take a third wife, yes, I would feel sorry for Queen Anne. Even if she would only suffer what she already did to Katherine.'

This was a long speech for Kit's mother and he pondered over what she had said. He still didn't really believe King Henry would put his lovely wife aside. Maybe he was just angry with her?

Kit remembered what his father had once said to him about one of the old men who had lost his head on Tower Hill the year before: 'The anger of the prince means death,' the Duke of Norfolk had told him, yet the old man had stood up to the king. That had been brave. Kit wondered if Queen Anne could stand up to the king's anger and what would happen to her if she did.

The birds travelled far and wide to bring back their information to the ravens, who passed it on to Kit. News was coming from the palace in Greenwich, the secretary's houses in Chancery Lane and Stepney, the house at Hatfield where both princesses Mary and Elizabeth were living, and it was not good.

'The king is putting the word about that the queen is a witch,' Bran told Kit, whose eyes grew round at this new development.

'Why?' he asked.

'So he can claim she bewitched him into marrying her and get rid of her more easily.'

'Get rid of her? You mean divorce her?'

'Let's hope that's all it means,' said Bran. And if a raven can look more grim than usual, this king among birds looked very grim indeed.

After that, everything seemed to happen very quickly; there was soon a name for the woman Henry hoped to make his next queen: Jane Seymour.

She had a brother at court. The queen was jealous of her and the king wanted her because she was quiet and not shrewish like Queen Anne.

Kit relayed all this to his parents. His mother shook her head. 'Now she really *is* in danger. The king does not like to be criticised or crossed. And if Anne has been difficult with him, he'll like a quiet woman for a change.'

'Being friendly with the king is like playing with a tame lion,' said the Ravenmaster. 'That's what Thomas More said. You never know when he is going to turn on you. And when he does, watch out for those teeth and claws.'

One evening at the end of April, a pigeon brought the ravens the worst news so far.

'It was sitting on the windowsill of the secretary's

dining room in Stepney,' said Bran. 'Cromwell was giving wine and good food to a young court musician called Mark and he started to question him about the queen.'

'A musician?' asked Kit. 'What does he know of witchcraft?'

'Well, he certainly found her enchanting,' said Bran. 'He told the secretary he had lain with her. And that he wasn't the only one!'

Kit was horrified. He didn't need Bran or anyone else to tell him that to be unfaithful as the king's wife was a serious accusation. And this king was not known for his mercy. Two old men who had relied on it were now without their heads.

Another bird flew in and landed on Bran and Blodwen's cage. It was a very spangly young starling and it bowed to the big black bird, then burst forth with such a glorious barrage of sound that Kit was sad he couldn't understand Starling. Bran translated for him:

'The king's household is in uproar. The king and queen were supposed to travel to France in a few days and now the king has cancelled their trip. All the packing has to be undone and all the travel arrangements stood down.'

Kit wanted to tell his father all he had learned but when the Ravenmaster found him as he was putting the ravens in their cages for the night, Thomas Wagstaffe looked white-faced.

'We have a new prisoner in the Tower, Kit,' he said.

'A young man arrested for crimes committed with the queen against the king's majesty.'

Kit swallowed. 'Is he called Mark?' he asked.

His father nodded. 'He is Mark Smeaton, the king's lute-player, and he is now in a cell in the Tower. And from what I've heard he won't be the last.'

It was time for Kit to find out more.

For the last few weeks, he had not trimmed the flight feathers of Huginn and Muninn. He had suspected he might need to send out his own special spies at some point and this was it. The pigeon had told Bran that the king would attend the joust at his palace in Greenwich the next day.

The next morning Kit was up early to feed the birds and after they had eaten, he looked carefully round and sent Huginn and Muninn off to Greenwich. It was quite safe to have them out of the way all day because the ravens always spread themselves around the Tower grounds until it was time to come back for more food in the evening. His father wouldn't notice the absence of two out of six. And if the Ravenmaster wouldn't, no one else would.

It was going to be a long day waiting for their news, so when he had finished cleaning the cages, Kit went to see Isabel. Her busiest time was first thing in the morning, so he had to wait until all the loaves and rolls had been taken out of the ovens and the many Tower warders and palace workers served before she was free to talk to him.

Their roles had been reversed lately, with Kit giving her the latest court gossip, but he didn't reveal his sources. Isabel was intrigued that he knew more than she had gleaned from women servants but Kit didn't want to tell her that his information came from pigeons and common sparrows.

Now she was eager to talk. 'Have you heard about the musician,' she asked straight away, 'and what they say he has done?'

Kit nodded. 'I am afraid for the queen,' he whispered.

'Do you really think a royal queen, the highest lady in the land, would lie with a mere lute-player?' Isabel whispered back.

They stared at each other in quiet amazement.

'I don't know,' said Kit. 'It seems very dangerous. I have no idea what ordinary women think, let alone queens. Could it be that the musician is very handsome and the king no longer pleasing in the queen's eyes?'

He felt his cheeks flaming at discussing such a thing with a girl, even one who was his good friend.

Isabel snorted. 'An "ordinary woman" might think like that but such thoughts in a queen could lead to serious consequences.'

'That is what I am afraid of,' said Kit.

Huginn and Muninn returned within minutes of each other and Kit gave them extra water and a hen's egg each, with its shell still on. Once they were refreshed they reported what they had seen at the tournament.

'The king was in a strange mood,' said Huginn. 'No

one expected him to take part – not after his accident in January – but he was in a wild and excited temper, cheering on all the combatants. And he had his horses with him, as if he might join in. He lent one of his best to a friend. But soon he drank deeply, called for a fresh horse and said he was leaving.'

'And he left the tournament?' asked Kit. 'Before it was over? And what about the queen?'

Muninn took up the tale. 'The queen was left behind. The king called over a companion, a fine gentleman – the one he had lent his horse to. I flew down to hear what he was saying. He said, "Norris, ride with me. I will back to Whitehall this instant." This man, Norris, obediently turned his mount and they left together, with only five other companions – but those others stayed back so the king and his friend could talk privately.'

'We flew down and followed them,' said Huginn, 'staying close enough to hear the conversation between the king and this Norris but high enough that they didn't notice us.'

'And what did they say?'

'The king accused Norris of lying with his wife,' said Huginn.

'With the queen,' added Muninn, just to be sure that Kit understood.

'Another one!' said Kit.

'Remember the lute-player said there were others besides himself,' said Bran, who was listening to the ravens' report.

'So you should expect another prisoner very soon,' said Huginn.

Kit went straight to his father to convey the latest news.

'Henry Norris?' said the Ravenmaster. 'But he is one of the king's closest personal servants! One of the innermost circle at court. If he is under suspicion, then anyone could be.'

And Huginn was right: by the next dawn Henry Norris was also a prisoner in the Tower. And he was not the last one for that day.

Before the sun went down Queen Anne herself entered through the Court Gate. Alerted by the ravens, Kit watched as she came in and was received by the constable.

He heard her shaky voice asking, 'Am I to be taken to a dungeon?'

She was clearly very frightened and looked as if she couldn't believe what was happening to her. Kit couldn't either.

At that moment, the queen looked up and caught his gaze. Kit knew she had recognised him and it seemed to give her courage to see someone she knew. She drew herself up to her full height (which was not great) and stepped inside the Tower. Even as a prisoner, she was still a queen.

4

The Queen's Man

The queen was not in a dungeon. She was settled in the same lodgings that had been decorated and prepared for her coronation three years earlier. She had five women with her but she sent for Alice Walsingham all the same.

Kit met the lieutenant's daughter outside the Queen's House. He had been drawn there in the hope of seeing again those bright black eyes, that smile which seemed to be only for him. Bran and Blodwen were pecking about on the green at his feet.

Alice was coming out of the door and beckoned to Kit to join her.

'She asked about you,' she told him. 'The queen looked out of the window and saw you. She called you the Young Raven!'

Kit's chest swelled. The queen knew who he was! He didn't mind 'Young Raven' – it was much better than George's contemptuous 'Bird Boy'. Kit had the strangest feeling that Queen Anne knew he could speak to the birds and understand them.

'What did you tell her?' he asked.

'Just your name and that the Ravenmaster and his wife took you in when your parents died,' said Alice. 'And that you are my friend.'

'How is she?'

'Very brave and cheerful,' said Alice. 'She laughs and jokes but then she weeps as well. I think she is very frightened.'

'I wish I could help her,' said Kit, clenching his fists. 'Can you tell her I am at her service? Will you see her again?'

Alice nodded. 'She has asked me to come each day. I don't think she trusts all her women. She couldn't say but I think she believes they are spying on her, even though two are her own aunts!'

Just then a warder arrived to escort Alice home.

'I must go,' she whispered. 'Meet me here at the same time tomorrow.'

The ravens had overheard everything.

'I shall go and sit on her windowsill,' said Bran.

'I should like to see the queen too,' said Blodwen.

Both of the big black birds flapped awkwardly up towards the queen's lodgings and Kit thought maybe he should stop trimming Bran's flight feathers too – he might need even more spies soon.

The birds quickly returned.

'There are five ladies waiting on the queen,' Bran said. 'And one is the constable's wife.'

'Lady Kingston?'

Bran bobbed his head to say 'yes'.

'So two are her aunts, another is the constable's wife . . . I wonder who the others are?'

'Can you ask your young lady-friend to find out for you?' asked Blodwen.

'I will,' said Kit. He didn't want to correct Blodwen about his relationship with Alice, because the new female was still a bit shy with him and hardly ever spoke to him directly.

He was beginning to think Alice had been right; it might just be a courtesy that the constable's wife was attending the queen, but she might also be spying for her husband. If so, the queen was more in need of a friend than ever.

He said as much to his father, who grew very alarmed.

'You are playing with fire if you try to get involved with the queen,' he said. 'I feel sorry for her too, but I think she is doomed.'

'You really think the king would have her . . . that she will die?'

'Ask yourself how many prisoners have left here lately with their heads on,' said the Ravenmaster.

'But a woman, and a queen!' Kit just couldn't believe it.

By the afternoon another prisoner had been thrown into a cell. It took Kit a while to find out who it was: the queen's brother, George, Viscount Rochford.

'That's three men,' said Isabel, as the evening drew in. 'All accused of the same crime with the queen.'

'But George Rochford,' said Kit. 'With his own sister? It makes no sense.'

'I hear you had a long conversation with Alice Walsingham?' said Isabel.

It seemed Kit wasn't the only one with spies.

'The queen asked for Alice to wait on her,' he said. 'And I wanted to know what was going on. I want to help her.'

'Oh, Kit,' said Isabel. 'You must be careful.'

'That's what my father says.'

But Kit was impatient for his meeting with Alice the next day, to find out if there was anything he could do to serve the queen, doomed or not.

'It's worse than we thought,' said Bran, when Kit went to feed him next morning. 'The plot is not just against the queen. A bunch of sparrows have told me they heard of a conspiracy to put the Princess Mary back ahead of little Elizabeth to succeed the king.'

'Can you really trust the news from sparrows?' asked Kit. 'They seem so . . . well, feather-headed, I suppose!'

'One sparrow and I wouldn't trust it,' said Bran, 'but you know I have spent hours fitting the story together from bits and pieces told by a whole flock of them.'

He seemed disgruntled, so Kit dipped some stale bread in a bucket of pig's blood he had begged from the butcher and fed the bird some grisly sops.

'I'm sorry, Your Majesty,' he prukked softly into the big bird's neck feathers. 'Of course I'm sure you are right. I just want to get all the facts straight.'

'One little group had flown a long way, from Hatfield,' said Bran. 'And they had listened at windows for some time when the Princess Mary met with people who promised her she would soon be ahead of her little half-sister in the succession.'

'With Elizabeth living in the same house?' said Kit. 'That was dangerous.'

'Can two-year-old humans suspect their sisters of anything so treacherous?' asked Bran. 'And I suppose her attendants didn't know the purpose of Princess Mary's visitors.'

Kit thought of the little princess toddling innocently about the house while her older half-sister listened to a plot to have her removed from any chance of one day being queen.

'But more sparrows have confirmed the plot,' Bran continued, nudging Kit for another bloody sop. 'They heard the same at the secretary's window.'

'Do they know who the conspirators were?' asked Kit.

'Sparrows don't know names,' said Bran. 'Their little heads are too small to retain human names. They can only say things like "the fat man" or "man with a thin beak". But I am quite sure about what they heard. They know "princess" because it's a word they like and "princess in black" was what they said.'

'Though we must call her Lady Mary now,' said Kit nervously.

'Not if the plot succeeds,' said Bran. 'She will be a princess again and in line to inherit the throne.'

'So what about the real princess?' asked Kit. 'The king and queen's daughter?'

'I would wager she will be the one called "Lady" next,' said Bran. And then he clacked his beak loudly. 'And that is if she is lucky.'

Kit was now thoroughly alarmed. If the sparrows were right, both the queen and the little princess were in danger.

He hurried through his morning tasks and went quickly to the queen's lodgings. All morning, ravens came and went, bringing Kit tidbits of information and checking that he was all right; it was a long wait. But eventually Alice came out on her own as she had done the day before. Kit took off his cap and gave a little bow. Her face brightened at the sight of him.

'Oh, Kit, I am so glad you are here,' she said. 'It is so terrible in there.'

'What is happening?' he asked. 'Is the queen in worse trouble?'

'Shh. Let's stroll towards the chapel,' said Alice. 'I'll be able to see when my escort comes.'

They walked across the green, three ravens keeping pace with them.

'How could she be in more trouble than being arrested for plotting against the king?' whispered Alice.

'What about the spies?' asked Kit, trying to look unconcerned.

'Two aunts the queen does not like,' said Alice. 'The constable's wife and the wives of two of the king's court servants. I have met them all now and they resent me. I have to pretend to be an ordinary young girl, chosen to visit the queen because of my innocence, to cheer her dark days.'

'And are you not that?' said Kit.

'No!' Alice forgot to lower her voice, then continued more quietly. 'Anne is the only queen I have known. I don't remember the old one and don't want a new one. You remember the coronation?'

'I do and I feel the same as you. My parents don't, though.'

'Nor does my father,' said Alice. 'He is trying to keep out of it and leave everything to the constable.'

She paced up and down the grass outside the chapel and Huginn and Thomas walked behind her, looking like sober councillors.

'Kit, are you willing to help the queen?'

'I am,' said Kit, and realised it was true. He was the queen's man, through and through.

'It will be dangerous,' said Alice, 'and you may have to do some bad things.'

'They will not be the first bad things to be done,' said Kit.

'Oh no,' said Alice. 'Here comes George. My father must have sent him to escort me. I don't know why he likes him so much.'

'Because his father is a nobleman, I suppose.'

'Hanging round Alice again, Bird Boy,' sneered George. 'Didn't you learn your lesson last time?'

But Kit just raised his hands and walked away, trusting that Alice would get a message to him now she knew his mind.

He bumped into Isabel before Alice and George were out of sight.

'Why does she have to have an escort from the green to her lodgings?' asked Isabel. 'You can see them from here!'

Kit shrugged. 'Her father insists. Alice doesn't mind going about on her own. She's quite brave actually.'

Isabel pulled a face. 'Is there any more news?'

Kit didn't think he should share Alice's confidences about the women spies but he told her what news the sparrows had brought.

'Poor little Bess,' said Isabel.

Thomas the raven qu'aarked in response to the name.

'He thinks you mean his mate,' said Kit.

'Sometimes I think those birds understand every-thing we say,' said Isabel, giving Kit a shrewd look. Kit wondered if he could trust her but there was no time to speak more as the baker caught up with them and hurried Isabel home. He was a burly, silent widower. Kit felt so grateful to have Marjorie. Neither Alice nor Isabel had a mother living.

*

And he was grateful again in the night when he woke screaming from one of his terrible nightmares, bathed in sweat. Marjorie was soon at his bedside with a damp cool cloth for his forehead.

The nightmares were not so frequent now but they were always the same: he dreamed of his first mother and father. He could smell baking bread. The dreams always began that way, with the delicious smell of new bread and his parents alive and well. Then it would change: the bread burned, the oven went out, there was nothing to eat. And his parents lay moaning and unable to look after him. Black pustules broke out over their faces and bodies and a terrible smell spread through the house.

Then there was a pounding on the door and it was flung open by two men with cloths wrapped over their faces. Kit always hoped that the dream would stop there, with fresh air flooding into the fetid house. But it never did. With a slow inevitability the men came and pulled his mother's body out on to their cart; then they came for him.

Kit tried to speak, to cry out that he was alive, but no sound would come out of his mouth. He tried to struggle with the two men who picked him up, even though in his real past, he hadn't had the strength to resist. He had been slung on to the cart as limp as any rag.

In the dream, the men threw him on top of his mother; no one had bothered to close her eyes, which stared glassily up at him from her blackened face. It was when the men went back for his father to throw on top of him that Kit started screaming in earnest.

'There, there, lad,' said Marjorie, wiping his face. 'Everything is well. That was only a dream.'

Kit clung to her, his heart pounding. It had been so real.

'Was it the old one?' Marjorie asked him gently. 'The usual?'

'Yes, it is always that one,' said Kit. 'And although it was only a dream, it did really happen, didn't it?' He had never had any other nightmare – what had he dreamed about before his parents died? He gave one shuddering sob, then felt his heart begin to slow to its accustomed beat.

'I'll bring you some warm spiced ale,' said Marjorie, stroking his wet hair. 'And I'll stay with you till you go back to sleep.'

Kit thought again how lucky he was. And he thought of the little princess who might soon be without her mother. Would she as good as lose her father too? Everyone knew how mean King Henry had been about Princess Mary once he decided he hadn't been lawfully married to the old queen. She had been stripped of her title and kept apart from her mother. The king never saw her now.

He fell asleep thinking of the little girl with red-gold curls and listening to Marjorie's tuneless humming.

The next day, Alice told him that two more men had been committed to the Tower, both accused of the same crime as the other three.

'They are called Brereton and Weston and were both members of the king's inner circle. Weston used to sleep in the king's bed.'

'In the king's bed, not the queen's?' said Kit.

'That won't save him now,' said Alice. She was white and trembling with fear. 'Oh, Kit, how shall the queen escape death? She swears she is innocent of all charges and has always been a faithful wife to the king. But she has enemies who would be rid of her – and the king might be one of them!'

'What can I do?'

'You remember I told you that you might have to do something bad?'

'Yes,' said Kit. 'Just tell me what.'

'You are friendly with the baker's daughter, are you not?'

'Isabel, yes,' said Kit, puzzled. This seemed a strange change of subject.

'You must tell her what has happened and ask if she would like to save the queen. Do you think she would?'

'Yes, I believe so,' said Kit.

'Then she must help us to put something in the manchet loaves to be sent up to the queen's lodging,' said Alice. 'The queen will know not to eat the bread but her women will eat it and they will be overcome.'

'You want me to posion the women waiting on the queen?' said Kit. 'Very well. I will do it!'

5

Serving the White Falcon

Mossy Meg's house was not far from the Tower; Kit and Isabel walked there in less than ten minutes. She didn't have anything as obvious as a shop – that would have been too dangerous. But the instructions from the queen, relayed by Alice Walsingham, made her place not hard to find.

Isabel had been uneasy about the whole thing.

'You know that some people are saying the queen's a witch?' she said. 'Surely if she knows where to buy charms and poisons, it shows those people are right?'

'It's all right,' said Kit. 'I can go on my own. All you have to do is put the stuff in the loaves you make for the queen's people. Will you do that? It will only make them sleepy – they won't be harmed.'

'Huh! That's what your Alice says,' said Isabel. 'I'm sure she believes what the queen told her. But suppose the powder is not what she said? We might kill all the ladies and guards and Queen Anne might escape!'

Kit didn't think that would be such a bad thing, but he tried to reassure his friend.

'It is just so that I can go in and speak with the queen,' he said. 'She has an errand for me to do. And I believe her. The powder is just for the manchet loaves you send up to the queen's lodgings. It would take a whole bakery's worth of loaves to knock out every guard in the Tower.'

In the end Isabel had insisting on going with him.

Now they were outside the very ordinary house, Kit's courage faltered. He had never met a witch, or wise woman, as Alice had described Mossy Meg. In a way, he would have preferred a tumbledown cottage with a tottering chimney and a black cat at the window; this was too ordinary. There was no bell or knocker on the plain wooden door. It was as if the person living within wanted to be as anonymous as possible and found only by visitors who were determined.

Kit drew himself up tall and rapped on the door with his knuckles.

After a while, it opened a crack and one very bright blue eye appeared at about the level of the third button on Kit's jerkin.

'Yes?' said a voice full of suspicion.

Kit recited his lesson. 'I am come from . . . Mistress Pembroke . . . with a message.'

The door opened further and a little woman appeared, but to Kit's surprise she was not old and wrinkled as a winter apple. She could have been a young girl, so small and slight she appeared. Her hair was dark and her skin very white; there was nothing mossy about her.

'Who's this?' she asked, nodding towards Isabel.

'She is my friend,' said Kit. 'We have come from the Tower. May we come in?'

The inside of Meg's house was as simple and wholesome as the outside. There was only one room on the ground floor, with a cupboard on one side of the hearth that would have concealed a twisting staircase up to the bedroom if the door hadn't been open.

There was a stove on the hearth and cupboards for food and pans at one end of the room near a door that Kit guessed opened on to a scullery and back yard; at the other there was a scrubbed wooden table and two chairs. The only thing that reassured Kit they had come to the right place was the shelves, with rows and rows of pots all neatly labelled in dark ink.

'Are you Mistress Twynho?' he asked, to be on the safe side.

The woman nodded. 'You don't need to tell me your names. It is better I don't know. What does Mistress Pembroke want? I know her need must be great.'

'She told me to ask for the sleeping powder,' said Kit. 'But it must be the one that can be baked into bread without tasting suspicious.'

Meg looked surprised. 'I thought she would have sent for something to ease her passing,' she said.

'You think she will die?' asked Isabel.

'I do not have the long sight,' said Meg. 'But that is

what people are saying in the streets. And the penalty for treason would be burning.'

Kit shifted uneasily. Just how did the queen come to know this woman?

But Meg was busying herself among her pots, pouring mixtures of powders into a cone of paper. She handed it to Kit but he motioned to her to give it to Isabel.

'I must be the one who puts it in the loaves,' said the baker's daughter.

The two women discussed the quantities needed while Kit looked nervously out of the window. Suppose the house were being watched? Perhaps the queen's association with the wise woman was known? Kit imagined himself and Isabel being marched back to the Tower under guard.

'I have no money to give you,' he said abruptly, embarrassed to admit it.

'I serve the queen,' said Meg. 'Come back if you need anything more.'

'Why did you say "Mistress Pembroke"?' asked Isabel on their way home.

'Alice told me to,' said Kit. 'It's what the queen called herself to Meg. She was Marquess of Pembroke before she was queen.'

The Tower of London was a city within the city; once through the gate and inside its massy walls, you found streets, shops and all kind of lodgings. You could walk around safely for weeks unaware of what went on inside some of the buildings.

There were cells in which prisoners could be chained in such a way that it was impossible for them to stand or lie down, and others containing instruments of torture, like the rack.

No prisoners refused to confess once their limbs were being stretched till their sinews cracked and their joints dislocated; they had to be taken to their deaths on litters or in wheeled chairs, helped on to the bonfires that would burn them or up the stairs to the scaffolds where they would hang. And that was if they were lucky.

And the walls of the rooms where the torturers did their grim work were so thick that the screams of the prisoners were unheard and the many people who lived inside the Tower walls went about their daily business without knowing what was happening just feet away from them.

But Secretary Cromwell did not intend the men accused with the queen to be tortured. Instead, he questioned them himself – which some people said was worse.

Kit saw him crossing the green the morning after he and Isabel had been to visit Mossy Meg and his heart nearly stopped within his chest. He knew that Isabel had made the batch of tainted loaves and that her father had taken them in person to the queen's lodgings. He was just waiting for Alice to open the window and signal that it was safe to come up.

But what if Thomas Cromwell was on his way to interrogate the queen? Kit realised fully for the first time what danger he was in when he saw the secretary's grim visage. The man stopped and rubbed a hand over his face and Kit saw that he was tired and weighed down by heavy burdens.

I wouldn't be the king's secretary for the world, he thought.

But the danger passed. Cromwell was on his way out of the Tower.

Almost as soon as his broad back disappeared down towards the Court Gate, Alice leaned out of the leaded window.

'Kit!' she called softly. 'The women are all asleep. Come up.'

All except the queen, he thought.

The warders guarding the lower door were no problem; they knew Kit, had known him from a scrawny boy, and accepted his explanation that he had come with a message from her father for Alice. Kit was a useful boy for errands and messages.

He climbed the wooden stairs with a mixture of excitement and fear; what he and Alice and Isabel had done already was enough to get them in very serious trouble. And he had no idea what he was going to be asked to do next.

Kit had never seen inside the queen's quarters, even though they had been mostly empty since the coronation. And now the door at the top of the stairs stood ajar and there was a sound coming from inside like the noises horses make in their stalls at night.

Cautiously he inched round the door and found a scene like something from a fairy tale.

Five women lay sprawled on chairs or settles, their mouths open and a range of snores coming from them as they slept soundly, their fine skirts disarrayed around them.

Alice stood in their midst like a princess awake among her sleeping courtiers but it was the figure by the window that drew Kit's gaze.

The queen turned and smiled at him.

She was much thinner than the last time he had seen her, her collar bones jutting out in the square-cut neckline of her dress. She wore no headdress and her dark hair was coiled into a coif at the nape of her neck. She looked as plainly dressed as any ordinary woman.

And yet to Kit, she was beautiful.

'Ah,' she said. 'Here is my young Raven Knight. You have done well, you and young Alice. And your accomplice in the bakery.'

'Your Majesty,' said Kit, bowing as low as he could.

'I won't be that for much longer – even if I still am,' she said. 'You may say "my lady" if you wish.'

'My lady,' repeated Kit and thought, *that is exactly what she is.* 'How can I serve you?'

'You offer so openly and so quickly, Raven Kit,' said the queen. She put her hand to her throat. 'But it is dangerous to serve me now.'

She looked at the sleeping women. 'Oh, not the way these court ladies serve me. They are all in someone's pocket – mainly the secretary's.'

She came towards Kit and he saw how sunken her black eyes were in her thin face. Kit reached into his jacket.

'My lady, I took the liberty of bringing you a wholesome loaf. I know you could not eat the others.'

To his surprise, the queen began to weep.

'Oh my Raven Knight,' she said, brushing her tears away and smiling on him like the sun after a short summer shower. 'If you only knew how many fine jewels and silks and satins my admirers have given me in the last ten years! And yet I say that no ring or bracelet – nay, not even my crown – has been given with more kindness, or received with more thanks. You are a good boy.'

She nibbled at a corner of the white loaf and drank some wine from a goblet on the oak table. Kit waited to find out what he had been summoned for.

It seemed to him that time had stopped in that room, with the snoring women and a fly buzzing at the window. For the rest of his life, whether long or short, he thought that he would know all his past and future as coming before and after this encounter.

If it felt unreal to Kit, waiting in the silence while the queen took a little food and drink, how must it seem to her? A few days ago she had been the king's consort, the highest lady in the land. And now she was a prisoner in the Tower, accused of treason and worse.

It seemed the queen had been thinking the same.

'These were my apartments at the coronation, Kit,' she said. 'You see all these devices of the king's rose and my white falcon?'

It was true that all the luxurious hangings were embroidered with these symbols as well as the initials 'H' and 'A' entwined. If the rumours were true, they would soon be replaced by 'H' and 'J' and the falcons pushed out by the gold wings of the Seymour family crest.

'Alice and I saw the procession at your coronation, my lady,' he said. 'And Isabel too. All the young people in the Tower were allowed to watch.'

The queen smiled. 'Then you are my connection with happier times, young raven. And may be again. The king may yet be merciful, don't you think?'

She laughed and then stopped abruptly. 'But we cannot rely on the king's mercy. We must plan for the worst.'

Kit thought again of the two old men. Queen Anne was wise enough not to rely on the tender aspect of the lion.

'I think you have secrets, Kit,' said the queen. 'As I do. Secrets, and memories and fears as we all do. But also special means of finding out what is going on. And of sending messages outside the Tower?'

Alice was looking at him expectantly. 'I do, my lady,' Kit answered.

'I shan't ask what they are,' said the queen. 'I know what it is like to want to keep some secrets safe.'

Kit thought about the accusations of witchcraft. But he felt differently about witchcraft since visiting Mossy Meg.

'What I am most afraid about is the fate of the princess,' said the queen. 'My daughter is as innocent as I am and should not suffer for whatever happens to me.'

Kit decided not to tell her about the plot to remove Princess Elizabeth from the succession to the throne.

'Can you find out for me if she is safe?' asked the queen. 'And keep me informed about her? Also,' she hesitated, 'if you hear anything about the king's . . . disposition towards her. He used to be so fond of her.'

She turned away, back to the window, to hide her face, Kit thought.

It must have cost her a lot to tell a mere commoner boy that she feared for her daughter by King Henry.

What kind of monster is he? thought Kit, *that she could even think such thoughts?*

'I . . . already have means of information from Hatfield, my lady,' he said, and was rewarded with an admiring look from Alice.

'You have news from Hatfield? Is Elizabeth well? Are her attendants loyal?' The queen seemed to brush a veil from her mind before continuing. 'Does Lady Bryan treat her well? And her sister Mary – is she kind?'

'I don't have many details, my lady,' Kit lied. 'I will send again.'

'Please do!' said the queen eagerly. She looked about

her distractedly. 'I have nothing to give you for your pains.'

'I need nothing,' said Kit. 'You can trust me as your loyal servant without reward.'

One of the women gave a great snort and her eyes fluttered open. Kit didn't know which one it was; the only one he recognised was Lady Kingston.

'Time to go,' said Alice.

'Thank you, Kit,' said the queen. 'Alice is right. Hurry away. And come again tomorrow – or as soon as you have news.'

Kit ran down the stairs faster than he had come up them. He must get back to the ravens and tell them what he needed to find out. This was a job for Huginn and Muninn – he couldn't rely on a flock of sparrows, whatever Bran said.

But first he hurried to see Isabel and tell her how well her baking had gone. He found her white-faced and anxious.

'Oh, Kit,' she greeted him. 'I should have guessed my father would have eaten one of the poisoned loaves. Will he be all right?'

She gestured behind her to where the baker lay snoring on a sack of flour.

'He will be fine,' said Kit. 'The ladies are already waking up. But we must think of a new way of getting the bread to the queen's quarters. We are going to have to do this again.'

6

A Traitor's Death

Early next day, Kit sent Huginn and Muninn out to Hatfield. A little flock of sparrows agreed to show them the way.

'They say it's about twenty miles,' said Bran. 'So you won't get a report back till late tonight.'

'You understand that this time we want news of the little princess?' Kit reminded them. 'But if you find out anything about the plot to make Lady Mary the king's heir, that could also be useful.'

As soon as they were aloft and flying over the north wall, Kit went to see Isabel. All the bakery loaves had been normal this morning and her father was much the same as always – perhaps a bit grumpier than usual.

'He woke up with a dreadful headache yesterday,' whispered Isabel. 'When the powder wore off. As if he'd drunk too much ale, he said. But he knew he hadn't.'

'I wonder if the queen's ladies had a headache too?' said Kit. He didn't want them to suspect anything. 'We need to give them more sleepy bread tomorrow. I should have news of the princess by tonight. Perhaps I could take it to them?'

Isabel looked at him curiously. 'There's more to you than meets the eye, isn't there? The way you get information from birds – no ordinary boy could do that. And then, how did the queen know that about you? How could she tell?'

'Perhaps she really is a witch,' said Kit quietly. He didn't want to think it, even though he had seen that witches came in different guises.

'Who's a witch?' said a coarse voice behind him. George. 'Not Alice, though she seems to have bewitched you.'

Kit had reverted to his old method of keeping out of George's way – avoidance – but it was hard to ignore him when he was right in front of Kit, thrusting his big red face at his victim.

'Good morrow, Master Atwood,' said Isabel sweetly. 'What can I get you?'

George was distracted and while Isabel was serving him, Kit slipped away. But he wished he hadn't been overheard wondering if the queen was a witch. He must be more careful. Since he was already doing all sorts of things he shouldn't, he didn't want to risk being arrested for treason.

He stopped and took a deep breath. No one would defend the queen. There was more likelihood of his being called as a witness, if she were charged on a count of witchcraft. His carelessness would be more of a danger to Queen Anne than to himself.

Still breathing deeply, he crossed the green to the queen's lodgings and waited to see Alice, hoping that George would not follow him. While he waited, he stepped into the chapel to calm his fears and feel the coolness of its thick grey walls.

Kit leaned against the tomb of an earlier lieutenant of the Tower. He'd been the one who rebuilt the chapel after a fire, before Kit was born, and he had included this handsome monument to himself. But Kit's father had told him that the tomb was empty: Sir Richard Cholmondeley had fallen out of favour with the king and resigned his position. He died soon afterwards and was buried elsewhere.

It seemed that it had always been dangerous to rely on the king's good opinion.

Kit sat in the chapel until his mind had stilled, wondering what the ravens would find out at Hatfield House. He said a quick *Ave Maria* then came out on to the green just in time to meet Alice.

'There you are!' she said, looking quickly around her.

'Is everything all right?' asked Kit. 'Are the ladies recovered? Isabel's father ate one of the loaves and woke up with a sore head later.'

'They are well and grumbling as usual,' said Alice. 'They resent waiting on the queen.'

'Even her family? Her aunts?'

'Especially them,' said Alice. 'They are afraid that

they will lose their positions because of the queen's disgrace. And I'm sure Lady Kingston tells the constable everything the queen says when she goes back to their lodgings at night.'

'What has she had to report since yesterday?'

'Only good things. The queen has asked for her priest – she wants to take communion.'

'It will be a comfort to her,' said Kit.

'Unless they try to twist it to mean she wants to confess to wicked deeds,' said Alice.

The queen had reached the point where anything she did or said could be turned against her.

'And she has written a letter to the king,' said Alice. 'She told me that she wrote it while the woman were still coming round after eating the sleepy loaves.'

'Did she say what was in it?'

'Only that she had told the king she was innocent of all the charges against her, and asked for forgiveness if she had been too quarrelsome a wife.'

'Will she be able to send it to him?'

'Well, it was all sealed before her women were properly awake. The queen gave it to a guard to take to Sir William. She didn't trust his wife to take it.'

'I hope it reaches the king,' said Kit, 'and that he believes her.'

He left Alice to her escort and went back to the ravens. He found Bran walking about on the grass near his lodgings.

'You look worried, Kit,' said the big bird.

'I am. Even with my help and having the network of birds out spying, it still all comes down to whether the king shows mercy.'

'And he is not well known for that,' said Bran.

'What will I do if the queen is found guilty?' said Kit.

'You will do nothing. There will be nothing you can do.'

Huginn and Muninn were very tired after flying the twenty miles to Hatfield and the same back. Being used to the confines of the Tower, it was a long flight for them and all they wanted to do was eat and roost in their cages.

Kit's father was working with him to put the birds away for the night, so Kit couldn't hear the ravens' news.

'Hugh and Moony seem a bit out of sorts,' said the Ravenmaster.

Kit prayed he wouldn't notice their untrimmed flight feathers.

'They ate their supper well enough,' he said. 'In fact they were very hungry,' he added truthfully.

'Well, we'd better keep an eye on them and see how they are tomorrow.'

'I'll stay and keep an eye on them if you like,' Kit offered.

'Nay, lad. Your mother will have your own supper on the table. We'd best get back.'

So, in an agony of frustration, Kit walked with his father back to their lodgings. He cursed himself for an ungrateful wretch: he had a home, loving parents and his freedom. If he wanted to walk out of the Tower he could. He was not rich and would never be a great man but he was likely to keep his head.

Unless this business with the queen got him into trouble. Kit knew that the penalty for treason for a commoner was much worse than simple beheading. Common traitors were hanged until they were half-strangled and then their insides were pulled out of them while they were still alive, before their heads were cut off and their bodies cut into four pieces. It wasn't justice but butchery.

'You're very quiet tonight, Kit,' said Marjorie as he ate. He had started to think for the first time about how the meat in his stew had been cut from a dead animal.

'I'm all right,' he said. 'Just thinking about treason.'

'That's not surprising with all the prisoners we have in the Tower at the moment,' said his father.

'They're all nobles, aren't they?' asked Kit. 'They won't be . . . I mean, if they are found guilty, they will just lose their heads.'

'Just!' said his mother. 'It's enough.'

Thomas Wagstaffe hesitated. He knew what thoughts were upsetting Kit.

'Not all, son,' he said as gently as he could. 'Mark the musician is not noble. He has got caught up in the affairs of greater people than himself and if he is found guilty, he would have to face the full sentence.'

Kit pushed his platter away, feeling sick.

'But the secretary is supposed to have promised him mercy,' said his father. 'So perhaps he won't be found guilty.'

'Can I go out for some fresh air?' Kit asked, and his parents let him go.

'Did you have to tell him that?' asked Marjorie. 'The lad is clearly upset.'

'I didn't like doing it, Marjorie love,' said Thomas. 'But when have we ever lied to him?'

Kit was glad of the cool air on his face. He was shaking with the horrors. He had never seen the musician but he was imagining the brutality of the full sentence for treason on the tender body of a young man. Mark Smeaton was only four years older than himself.

He crossed the inner ward and the green, looking at where a candle burned in the window of the queen's lodgings, and was soon back at the raven cages.

He prukked softly outside the bars and a very sleepy Huginn responded.

'We thought you wouldn't come tonight,' the raven grumbled.

'Are you too tired to tell me what you found out?' said Kit. 'We can wait till the morning if you like.'

Though he knew he would not get a wink of sleep if he didn't know the ravens' news.

'It's all right,' clucked Muninn. 'But we must talk softly and not wake the others.'

'The main news,' said Huginn, 'is that the whole royal household is moving to Hunsdon.'

'Where is that?' asked Kit, alarmed that the princesses would move out of reach of his spy network.

'Not too far,' said Muninn. 'A few miles east of Hatfield. The king has another great house there.'

'But why are they moving?'

'I don't know,' said Huginn. 'We just found the household in disarray, with servants packing up goods and the princesses' attendants issuing orders for the move.'

'Did you hear any more news? Is the little Princess Elizabeth well?'

'She was shedding tears for the ball that her nurse took away to pack,' said Muninn. 'But she is well. A pretty little human, as humans go. Even though her feathers are such an outlandish colour.'

'She has the same feathers – I mean hair – as the king,' said Kit. 'What of the other princess – Lady Mary, I should say – is there any more news of the plot around her?'

Huginn and Muninn opened their beaks wide and clacked them softly as if they were yawning.

'We saw no conspirators,' said Muninn. 'I suppose it was not likely with all the house in uproar. I hope you don't want us to fly to Hunsdon tomorrow.'

'No,' said Kit. 'I will ask you for more details tomorrow morning, so I can tell the queen. Sleep now. You have done well.'

Next morning he went early to the bakery after feeding the ravens and letting them out of their cages. Huginn and Muninn walked with him across the grass, taking flying hops only when they reached cobbles.

Isabel had explained to her father that Kit had been asked to do the queen's bread delivery. That meant he was going to have to do it every day, whether or not he had tainted loaves to deliver.

Alice was surprised when he entered the queen's rooms with his basket but Kit kept his head down, trying not to catch Queen Anne's eye. He managed to whisper to Alice that he would be back later.

When he came back, the guards had changed so it was easy enough to say he had forgotten to take the basket away. The women were sprawled asleep as before and the queen eyed them cynically as Alice let Kit in.

'Look at them! My Boleyn aunt, my Shelton aunt, the constable's wife and two women whose husbands depend on the king for their titles and living. They are missing good tidbits of gossip to take back to their masters.'

Kit couldn't imagine anyone in his small family taking someone else's part against him. But then everything about his life was so different from the queen's that he put that thought from his mind.

'I have news, my lady,' he said.

The queen turned to him, her dark eyes bright with eagerness.

'Yes, tell me! How is my daughter?'

'She is well, according to the report I have had. She and the Lady Mary are moving to Hunsdon with their households. But the Princess Elizabeth is in good health and well looked after.'

'Thank you,' said the queen, taking a lacy handkerchief to her eyes. 'Will you send to Hunsdon for me? I need to know she continues well. She is not yet three, you know.'

Kit knew. He also knew that queens and other fine ladies did not look after their own little children but sent them away to live with others and to be tended by servants. But he could see how much Queen Anne loved her daughter and how afraid she was for her.

'I wonder how he would have behaved if Elizabeth had been a boy,' said the queen, but she was talking to herself, not to Kit and Alice.

She gave herself a little shake and stood up straighter.

'The safety of the princess is now my main concern,' she said. 'If . . . if anything happens to me, I want to know what arrangements have been made for her. Can you do that for me, my Raven Knight? I'm sorry if it puts you in any danger.'

'I will do everything I can,' said Kit.

There was a harsh 'Qu'aark!' from the windowsill.

'It's the ravens,' said Kit. He crossed to the lattice and opened it.

'They say they will answer any questions you want to ask, my lady. They are the ones who saw the princess.'

And for the next half-hour he acted as interpreter between the two big black birds and the queen, while Alice looked on in admiration.

7
The Poet

'More arrests,' said Kit's father, when he got back home.

'More men accused with the queen?' asked Kit. 'This is beyond belief. Who are they?'

'That's the trouble. One is called Sir Richard Page and I know nothing of him,' said the Ravenmaster. 'But the other is the poet, Thomas Wyatt, and he was once an admirer of the queen's when she was younger.'

'Won't we run out of places to put them all?' said Kit.

'The Tower has many rooms. It's more that we might run out of guards to watch them and servants to bring them food and water. Apart from poor Mark Smeaton, they are all noblemen and have to be treated more like guests than prisoners.'

'I could help,' said Kit. 'I could help look after the poet, if you like. Take up his meals and his shaving water.'

'Well, the poet wears a beard but I'll ask if you can

wait on him,' said the Ravenmaster. 'As long as it doesn't upset your work with the birds.'

Kit grinned. He knew how much the ravens would hate being referred to as 'birds'. But he hoped that if he could get into the cell of one of the accused men, he might find out something that could help the queen. Would she be distressed about the arrest of this man she had once known? Kit wondered whether to tell her.

It was evening before he met the poet. Guards let Kit through the outer door and he carried up the stairs a basket with a meal that had been hot when it left the Tower kitchens.

Another guard he knew by sight unlocked the cell door. The poet was standing by the small slit window but turned at the sound.

He was a tall and handsome figure, outlined in the fading light from the window.

'Who's this?' he said, moving closer to inspect Kit and his basket.

'I'm Kit. I've brought your dinner.'

'And some wine, I see,' said the poet. 'I am more interested in that than in the food. Being imprisoned has taken my appetite away.'

Kit only had a few minutes; the guard would get suspicious if he stayed long with the prisoner. He poured him a cup of wine.

Then he said, 'Would you like me to take a message to the queen?'

Thomas Wyatt spilled his wine on the flagstones.

'What? You are waiting on Anne?'

'Not officially,' said Kit. 'But I am helping her when I can.'

Thomas Wyatt gave him a long appraising look.

'I think there is more to you than meets the eye, Kit.'

Kit wondered what it was about him that made everyone say that; he must look very ordinary and dull indeed if he kept surprising people this way.

'There must be nothing in writing,' said Wyatt. 'Nothing that could be found and get you – or the queen – into trouble.'

He paced up and down, his wine forgotten.

'Just say to her, "Caesar's you are still." Can you remember that?'

'I can,' said Kit.

'And tell her not to worry about me. Cromwell is my friend. And come again, if you can.'

The guard put his head round the door. 'Are you coming out, boy?'

Kit hastily unpacked a still faintly warm pasty from his basket, together with a linen napkin, some cheese and two rather withered apples.

'Do eat, if you can, sir,' he whispered, then backed out of the cell as quickly as he could.

'Off his food, is he?' asked the guard. 'Not surprised. I would be too if my head was going to be taken from my shoulders.'

'You really think he will be executed?'

The guard shrugged. 'Who knows? Will they kill the queen and seven men just so's the king can get him a new wife?'

It seemed that was the question in everyone's minds inside the Tower walls. Kit had never known his home – a place of safety to him – to be so full of tension and fear.

And behind it all was the figure of the king, the wounded lion who could kill with one lash of his mighty paw or snap of his jaws.

'But he's not lying wounded, is he?' said Isabel that evening. 'I've heard he's off every night wooing Jane Seymour. That doesn't sound like a man with a broken heart to me.'

Kit wondered how the king could do it. How he could be paying court to his next wife while his present wife still lived. It did not seem to be a good omen for Queen Anne.

'But perhaps she doesn't have to die,' Kit said. 'Sometimes she tells Alice that she hopes the king will let her go into a nunnery.'

'And she knows that will get back to the king through the constable and his wife,' said Isabel. 'She is clutching at straws, just hoping to let him know she would agree to that.'

'What do you think will happen to the princess if the queen does . . . if she doesn't survive?'

'Well, she won't be a princess any more. She'll be Lady Elizabeth, the way Princess Mary is now

Lady Mary. She's so young it probably won't make any difference to her.'

But Kit couldn't help fearing that would not be all that would happen.

Next morning he took hot water up to the poet so that he could wash.

'Ah, young Kit,' said Thomas Wyatt when he saw him.

'I have not been able to deliver your message yet, sir,' said Kit quietly. 'But I have remembered it and it will go to the queen today.'

'You are a good boy,' said the poet. 'One who can be trusted.'

He washed his face and hands. Kit saw that his supper had disappeared.

'I will be back with some breakfast for you very soon,' he said.

Kit had to race to catch Alice before she went up to the queen.

'If you get the chance, can you give the queen a message from the new prisoner?' he asked. 'I won't see her today.'

'Do you mean the poet?' asked Alice. 'I heard he was in the Tower.'

'He is and I have been been waiting on him,' said Kit. 'Can you say "Caesar's you are still" to the queen? But only if you will not be overheard. Oh and say Thomas

Wyatt told her not to worry about him – Secretary Cromwell is his friend.'

'She has been getting me to help with her clothes,' said Alice. 'And her women take no more notice of me than if I had been a stool. So it should be easy enough.'

'Come to the window and wave if you have succeeded in giving her the message,' said Kit. 'And I'll meet you when you finish here, in case there is a message for me to take back to him.'

Alice looked at him curiously.

'Be careful, Kit,' she said and leaned over to kiss him on the cheek.

Kit's face burned. 'You too, Alice,' he said.

He had to walk up and down the green several times after that. Bran walked behind him, serious as a judge.

But he couldn't spend all morning waiting for Alice and wondering why she had kissed him.

When there was nothing the ravens needed, Kit was expected to do chores about the house and help his father with other tasks that were part of his work as a Yeoman Warder. Today's job was cleaning harnesses for the many horses stabled in the Tower.

It was a good time to talk, rubbing fat into the leather of bridles and saddles.

'What do you think of our poet?' said the Ravenmaster. 'We've never had a poet in the Tower – not in my time.'

'I like him,' said Kit. 'He's a gentleman.'

'Well, we've had a lot of those!'

'I don't mean he's a knight or has any other title. I mean he's . . . I don't know . . . sort of naturally good.'

'That's what you learn as you get older, Kit. How to tell a man's character.'

'And a woman's?'

'You are thinking of the queen.'

Kit hadn't told his father that he had met the queen in her lodgings and was acting as her spy.

'I *was* thinking of her,' he said. 'She seemed so charming when they came with Blodwen. And yet they are saying all these terrible things about her.'

Thomas rested his arms over the big saddle he was oiling.

'It is not just her . . . well, her morals, people are talking about,' he said quietly. 'There are rumours that she poisoned Queen Katherine.'

Kit remembered what a supporter of the old queen his father had been. But he was still shocked. Witchcraft was one thing, especially since he'd met Mossy Meg, but murder?

'And that she was plotting to do away with Princess Mary – to make the way clear for herself as the only queen and her daughter as the only princess.'

'There must be a lot of people who hate her, to say such things,' said Kit.

He wondered if these were the same people who were plotting to restore Lady Mary's right to inherit the throne. But he couldn't let his father know about that either.

'I can't tell you whether they hate her or just know something we don't,' said the Ravenmaster. 'You can't trust that she is a good woman just because she has a charming manner and sparkling black eyes, Kit.'

Kit longed to say that the queen loved her daughter and wanted her kept safe but he realised that it didn't mean she was not capable of murdering another woman's child. He was beginning to understand that goodness and wickedness were more complicated than he used to think.

'I know it's not about how she looks or her manners,' he said eventually, when the silence had stretched out uncomfortably between them for too long.

'And you have to ask yourself if she behaved well in agreeing to marry the king when he already had a wife,' said the Ravenmaster.

'That's what Mother thinks,' said Kit. 'But perhaps the king was so determined that she had to give in. He *is* the most powerful person in the land, after all.'

Then he remembered something else.

'And isn't Jane Seymour doing the very same thing? Letting him court her while he is still married to Anne Boleyn?'

Thomas sighed. 'I can't argue with that, Kit. But if Jane Seymour becomes the next queen, we will have to bow to her, just the way we had to when Anne replaced Katherine. You are right. When you come down to it, everyone has to do what the king wants.'

*

Alice was flushed when she came down from the queen's lodgings. The escort sent to accompany her back home was used now to Kit's presence and let them have a few minutes alone.

'I did it!' said Alice. 'I gave her the message from the poet.'

'And is there a reply?'

'Yes, but I don't understand it. She laughed and then wept a bit, the way she does. Then she said, "Poor Thomas! I hope his faith in the secretary will be justified. I thought he was my friend once, too." Then she wrung her hands together and said, "Tell him that the thunder ever rolls around the throne and I am like to be struck by lightning." What do you suppose that means?'

'I don't know,' said Kit truthfully. 'But I expect the poet will. You are sure those were her very words?'

'Yes. Exactly as I have told them to you. But I couldn't ask what she meant because I had no more time alone with her. The women are always watching and listening.'

'How is she?' asked Kit.

'The same as before. Have you any more news for her?'

Kit shook his head. 'Not yet. But I am going to continue delivering her bread. Isabel has arranged it.'

Alice looked at him curiously. 'You and Isabel are very good friends, aren't you?'

'Yes, we have known each other for nine years,' said Kit.

He was only being honest but a small frown appeared between Alice's brows.

'Do you think she is pretty?'

'Isabel?' asked Kit. He was still thinking of the queen. 'I don't know. I suppose so.'

Alice looked as if she was on the verge of asking more but her escort was getting impatient for his dinner. So she just gave Kit a tight little smile and turned away.

By the time he took the poet his supper, Kit had rehearsed the queen's message so many times that it bubbled out of him as soon as he was inside the cell.

'Slow down, boy,' said Thomas Wyatt. 'I can hardly understand you. Say it again. You say she said "Poor Thomas" first?'

'Yes,' said Kit, pouring the poet's wine. 'And that she hoped you were right about Secretary Cromwell. She had thought him her friend once.'

'They have quarrelled,' said the poet. 'That is what all this is about. If he were still her friend, Anne would not be in the Tower now.'

Kit was beginning to understand that there might be one person in England almost as powerful as the king.

Thomas Wyatt drank his cup of wine in one gulp.

'And then she spoke of thunder and lightning?'

Kit repeated more slowly what Alice had told him.

The poet smiled and then put his head back and laughed, showing his white teeth above his beard.

'She is quoting an old Latin tag, as if she were a poet herself,' he said. 'I might use it in my own verses one day – it is certainly as true today as when it was written.'

'What does it mean?' asked Kit, then thought he might have been too bold. 'I mean if you want to say. It isn't my business.'

'Oh but it *is* your business,' said the poet. 'We have both used you and put you in danger. It is only fair to tell you what our exchange meant.'

He walked the small distance between the walls of his cell while Kit busied himself with the supper.

'I loved her, Kit,' said Thomas Wyatt softly. 'She was my beloved, the lady of my heart. And then the king saw her.'

Kit felt sorry for him.

'When the king sees a woman he likes, all other admirers must give up their claim. I yielded to him . . . I wrote some poems about it too. Oh, I didn't make it too obvious who they were about but the first one made it clear that I would not pursue the woman who belonged to "Caesar" or the king.'

'So that was why you sent that message?'

'But she replies using an image about how dangerous it is to approach the throne. That there is always thunder in the air around a king.'

'And she fears the lightning,' said Kit.

'She fears death,' said the poet. 'As we all do. And the secretary is no longer her friend. She is right to be afraid of the coming storm.'

8
A Plot

Kit's life was getting busier than ever. After helping his father feed the ravens in the morning, he ran down to the palace bakery to collect a basket of loaves to take up to the queen's lodging. Then he rushed back to take Thomas Wyatt his breakfast and hot water before doing his other chores.

By the time Kit met Alice coming down from waiting on the queen, he was worn out and full of little bits of information that stuck to him like burrs, picked up as he moved around the Tower.

One of the burrs on this day was particularly worrying.

'The grand jury has fixed the date for the trial of the men,' he whispered to Alice. 'Has the queen heard?'

'She didn't say anything,' Alice whispered back. 'When will it be?'

'On Friday.'

'So soon?' Alice looked shocked. Friday was only two days away.

'They said there was enough evidence for a trial,' said Kit.

'How many men?'

'Four – Smeaton the musician, Weston, Norris and Brereton.'

'But not the poet?'

'Not yet. I don't know anything about Richard Page but Thomas Wyatt is safe so far – there will be more trials, I'm sure. Nothing has yet been said about the queen or her brother.'

'You are sure they will be tried too?' asked Alice.

'Yes,' said Kit and realised for the first time that he had given up hope of saving the queen. Once she came to trial there would be nothing he could do.

He sat down heavily on a bench.

'What is it, Kit?'

'How can we save the queen?' he said. 'The only way would be if we could smuggle her out of the Tower to safety. But how could we do that? Even with your help and Isabel's, we are just three young people against a body of armed guards and the will of the king and his secretary.'

'Don't despair. The queen is depending on us to do what we can. Look, bring sleepy loaves tomorrow so we can tell her about the men's trial in case she hasn't heard. We can be there to support her.'

'But we must have something good to tell her as well,' said Kit. 'I'll send the ravens to Hunsdon to see if there is any good report of the little princess.'

*

In a room in a grand house in the fashionable part of town a nobleman was deep in conference with his steward.

'You say you know men fit for the task?' said the lord.

'Yes, my lord. They are lacking in principles but reliable enough to do the deed.'

'And do they understand that they will have no support from anyone if they are caught or if the attempt is botched?'

'They do, my lord. The large sum of money they are getting is enough assurance for them.'

'And they do not know your name? They could not trace you to my employment?'

'They know me as Arthur Burford and have seen me only masked. I was of course not wearing Your Lordship's livery.'

The lord chuckled. 'Arthur Burford? That is very thorough of you.'

He walked to the window, disturbing a robin who was pecking about on the sill.

'How many men?' he asked.

'Three.'

'For one small girl,' said his lord. 'It should suffice.'

'They will be heavily armed, because there will be some sort of guard about the princess.'

The robin on the windowsill had been joined by a couple of starlings.

'I think the king has not provided a very heavy guard at Hunsdon?' said the lord.

'Not more than these men can cope with,' said his steward. 'Surprise is everything, after all.'

'And those who wait on the real princess will not put up a fight,' said the lord. 'Though she must know nothing of the attempt.'

'She will not, my lord.'

'She is too soft-hearted,' said the lord, musing aloud to himself. 'She knows only that we work for her restoration. She would not give us her approval for any violence on the royal bastard. But this is the only way to be certain.'

'And the secretary, my lord? Is he to know?'

'Not until we have succeeded. And even then I must forgo the pleasure of his knowing who was behind it. I am not convinced that he wants what we do.'

The steward smiled. Of course it was flattering to be included in his lord's group of intimates who were working for Anne Boleyn's downfall and the restoration of the Princess Mary. If they only knew he despised all lords and was just biding his time.

With the success of this plot – or of some other – he would have his lord exactly where he wanted him. 'Arthur Burford' did not intend to remain a steward for ever.

Huginn and Muninn had been sent off on their errand and Kit had gone to tell Isabel that they would need another batch of tainted loaves to take to the queen the next morning.

He had a few minutes to himself in which to munch on a cheese pasty Isabel had slipped him, when a harsh 'Qu'aark' from a nearby tree alerted him to Bran's presence.

'Good afternoon, Your Majesty,' said Kit, in Raven, and the big black bird landed awkwardly at his feet. The ravens, so magnificent in flight, always looked like old men with sore feet when they went about on the ground.

'I have had another report from the birds,' said the King Raven. 'It may be nothing but I thought you should know.'

Kit gave him a piece of his pasty and Bran put back his neck to let it slip down his throat.

'Tell me,' he said.

'A robin and two starlings, all saying the same – that they had paid attention to the word "princess" in a grand house in town. As they listened, they also heard the word "Hunsdon" and they thought there was a plot being hatched against the little princess.'

'They were sure they heard "Hunsdon"?' asked Kit.

'Yes, and they didn't know about the earlier information so they can't have made up a story about it.'

'Did they say what sort of plot?'

'Only that it had to be kept very secret. The robin thought that "three men" had been paid a lot of money to do something.'

'And any word of when?'

'Birds don't really know dates,' said Bran.

'Could they find the house again?'

'I asked them that and they said they could. I think I should go there with them as soon as my flight feathers are long enough.'

Kit gave Bran the rest of his pasty; he wasn't hungry any more. He hoped the other ravens would bring him better news to give the queen the next day. He didn't want to tell her any of this.

Huginn and Muninn came back tired again from their long flight but this time Kit managed to meet them before his father came out to feed the ravens. He had a few tidbits stored inside his jerkin to give them.

'Do you find it?' he asked. 'Did you reach Hunsdon?'

'It was easy to find,' said Muninn. 'There is a huge tower – taller than anything here – and we perched on the weathervane on the very top of it, to recover from the flight.'

'Then we divided up the space and went on our separate ways,' said Huginn. 'I to look in through the gallery windows and Muninn to spy through the first floor windows of the royal apartments. We did not want to alarm anyone with the sight of two ravens together and there were many windows to look through.'

'It sounds like a very grand house,' said Kit.

'It is,' said Muninn. 'Every part of it is ornamented and gilded with the king's symbols and great beasts.'

Kit thought about Anne's white falcon and wondered if even now, carpenters and gilders were being commissioned to carve many pairs of angel wings in readiness for another queen, replacing the Boleyn arms with the Seymour ones.

'Did you see the princesses?' he asked. 'Had they moved from Hatfield?'

'They had,' said Huginn. 'Both princesses and their attendants. The little one was playing with a ball all along the great gallery and Muninn saw her older sister supervising the unpacking of her dresses in the royal bedchambers.'

'That sounds good,' said Kit. So neither princess was in fear or distress yet. 'But I think the little Elizabeth is in danger,' he said.

And he told the ravens what news Bran had brought to him from the city.

'What sort of guard has the house in Hunsdon?' Kit asked.

The ravens shook their glossy wing feathers.

'Not many men,' said Huginn. 'And they were all at the gatehouse.'

'Where the great carved beasts are,' added Muninn.

'Well, wooden beasts won't protect the princess,' said Kit. 'Even if they are lions and wolves. Would it be easy for a gang of ruffians – say three armed men – to break in through the walls somewhere else?'

The ravens looked at each other with their large black eyes and a silent communication went between them.

'I think it would not be difficult to get inside the grounds,' said Huginn.

'We've got to do something,' said Kit. *I've* got to do something.'

But what he had to do next was feed the ravens and then take the poet his supper.

'I shall see the queen again tomorrow morning,' he told Thomas Wyatt, as he unpacked the poet's food. 'Though I don't know what I am to tell her. It seems as if there is bad news at every turn.'

'What sort of news?' asked Wyatt.

'Well, you know that four men are to face trial the day after tomorrow?'

'I had heard.'

'They were all her friends,' said Kit. 'And it doesn't seem likely that they will be found innocent.'

'They were the king's friends too,' said Wyatt. 'Except Smeaton. He is too lowly to have been friend to king or queen.'

'You don't believe what they are saying about the queen and these men?' asked Kit.

The poet gave him a stern look.

'I do not,' he said. 'Anne was always a merry lady and some of her jests could go too far. But she is honest, and true to the king. If she should die, her guilt would have nothing to do with it.'

'You still love her?' whispered Kit, realising that this must be true.

The poet sank on to his hard bed with a sigh.

'I do, Kit. Oh, I have a wife and a son. I was married even before the king took Anne from me.

But I am not happy. I have not been happy since I lost Anne.'

'Just a minute,' said Kit.

He went to the guard, who was a young warder Kit knew well and told him that the poet had asked for his company while he ate.

'Just knock on the door when you are ready to leave,' said the guard.

Kit went back to Thomas Wyatt.

'You must eat something,' he said. 'Look, here is roast chicken and a meat pie. I will pour you some wine.'

The poet rubbed his hands across his face.

'Thank you,' he said, taking the cup. 'It is good of you to take care of me. I won't forget you when I leave here.'

Kit noticed that he was still thinking in terms of 'when' not 'if'. Secretary Cromwell must be a good friend to him indeed.

'It is a good sign that you have not been called to trial, sir,' he said.

'It is not that I am in danger that makes me sad,' said Wyatt. 'But what was your other bad news?'

Kit wondered how far to trust him.

'The queen asked me to find out about her daughter,' he said slowly. 'And I think the princess might be in danger.'

'Tell me,' said Wyatt. 'If I can be of help, I will.'

So Kit told him everything, even about the birds, even the ravens.

'And you don't know who this lord is?' he said. 'Could the ravens take you to his house?'

Kit realised that they could and that it would be both necessary and very dangerous.

He spent a restless night, finding sleep escaped him. Every time he closed his eyes, he saw a vision of a little girl with red-gold curls toddling along after a rolling ball. Then men came and struck down her attendants and carried the little girl off, screaming, in a sack.

He had no doubt that the plan was to kill her. It would not be difficult to snuff the life out of a girl-child of less than three years. But how exactly would the men do it? The more he thought about it, the more sickened he became.

In the end he gave up and re-lit his candle. He made a list of all that he knew about the plots against Princess Elizabeth and in favour of the Lady Mary.

It was precious little. He knew no names or dates and only two locations: Hunsdon and wherever the lord lived.

Then there was what he could do about it. The poet had made one suggestion but it was so terrifying that Kit thought he should try anything else first. He watched the paper with his list on it burn in the candle flame.

Kit dragged himself out of bed early next morning, feeling like a piece of meat chewed by a raven. His father looked at him and sent him off to the bakery.

'I'll feed the birds,' he said. 'You are exhausting yourself with all your extra tasks.'

The queen was getting thinner, even though Kit always made sure she got a wholesome loaf on the days that Isabel contaminated the bread.

'You are going to have to go back to Mossy Meg,' Isabel told him when he collected today's basket. 'I am running out of the powder.'

That was just another job for Kit to fit into his busy day. He took the poet his breakfast and washing water and told Wyatt that the queen was very thin.

'She was always slender,' said Wyatt. 'Not a buxom woman.'

'Now she is wasting away,' said Kit. 'Even if the king were to spare her, I think she would die anyway.'

'Have you thought any more about what I suggested?' asked the poet.

Kit nodded. 'It kept me awake. That and what will happen to the princess if I do nothing.'

He left the Bell Tower and went to find Bran.

'Could you take me to the lord's house?' he asked the raven. 'Could you show me where he lives?'

'Well, I could try,' said Bran. He spread his wings. 'What do you think of my feathers? It would be a short flight. Not like going all the way to Hunsdon.'

'Could we try this afternoon?' asked Kit.

'I can send word to the robin and starlings,' said Bran. 'They could lead me and I could lead you. But you must be careful.'

So when Kit went back to the queen's lodgings, he had a plan, even though he couldn't tell her about it.

He picked his way round the sleeping women and went to kneel to the queen. She put her hand on his head.

'Rise up, Sir Kit!' she said, laughing. 'My Raven Knight! What news?'

'You are merry, my lady,' said Kit. 'I am glad to see you so well.'

'Well, what am I do?' she said. 'I am a prisoner, am I not? If I cannot laugh and jest, then I am a miserable one.'

Kit swallowed. 'You have heard about tomorrow's trial?'

'Oh yes, Lady Kingston was very careful to inform me,' said the queen. 'Tell me, Kit, are they laying bets in the Tower? And is anyone putting good money on my courtiers walking free from their trials and leaving the Tower alive tomorrow?'

There was nothing Kit could say to this so he did not stay long with the queen.

9

The Secretary's Face

That afternoon, Kit strolled out of the main gate, and dawdled round the streets near the Tower until a harsh cry from the air above alerted him to Bran's presence. The black bird flapped lazily behind some smaller ones and they set off, heading west.

Kit would soon have been lost in the tangle of alleys that lay under the birds' direct flight but it was not long before they came out into an area of big houses several storeys high and full of windows – a sure sign that their owners were wealthy men.

Bran landed on the roof of one.

Kit stood on the other side of the road, aware as never before that he was not the kind of person who would be admitted to a grand house. He had washed his face and hands but he couldn't remember when he had last combed his hair; his mother was always nagging him about it.

His clothes were decent but made of homely stuff

and he knew that this lord's visitors would wear satin and velvet.

Bran qu'aarked and flew down to a windowsill on the first floor. He cocked his head and looked like a grave counsellor considering his options. It gave Kit heart.

Perhaps I don't have to go inside, he thought. *Maybe it's enough to know where the lord lives.*

But that was just the trouble. Kit didn't know where he was and he doubted that he'd be able to find his way here from the Tower again without Bran's help. So how could he identify the lord? He knew that not even Bran could tell him the lord's name unless he heard somebody speak it.

Just then a messenger, much better dressed than Kit, came and knocked at the front door. A liveried servant appeared and took a piece of paper from the boy's hand.

Kit crossed the road to get within earshot.

'Are you to wait for an answer?' the servant was asking the messenger.

The boy shook his head.

The servant gave the boy a small coin and closed the door again. The messenger was setting off back the way he had come when Kit gathered up his courage and stepped into his path.

'I'm sorry to detain you,' he said politely, 'but could you tell me whose house that is?'

The boy looked astonished to be spoken to. He was not much older than Kit, red-haired and with a rash of freckles over his nose and cheeks.

'Who wants to know?' he asked cautiously.

'Kit – Kit Wagstaffe, from the Tower of London.'

Kit stuck out his hand and the boy took it, his eyes round as florins.

'The Tower?' he said. 'That's a dangerous place to live at the moment.'

'Not if you look after the ravens,' said Kit. He called up to Bran, who flew down and sat on his shoulder.

The boy looked at him with respect.

'That is a sight to see,' he said, eyeing Bran's huge black beak and the talons that gripped Kit's padded jerkin. 'Is he tame?'

'Not at all,' said Kit, 'but he knows me.'

'Oh but where are my manners?' said the boy. 'I am Will – William Rede – from the household of Thomas Cromwell.' He made a nervous little bow, as much to the raven as to Kit.

'The secretary?' said Kit, his heartbeat quickening. But he liked the look of Will Rede.

'Yes,' said Will proudly. 'And he sent me with a message to Lord—'

'Wait a moment,' said Kit, looking left and right. 'Is there somewhere quiet we could go to talk?'

He had to find out why the secretary was communicating with the lord. If Cromwell knew about the plot against the princess, then all was lost.

Mossy Meg was grinding powders with a pestle and mortar when Kit knocked on her door. It was late afternoon.

'You haven't brought the maid this time?' said Meg, looking behind him.

'No,' said Kit, 'yet it is Isabel who has sent me. She needs more of the sleepy powder to mix into the bread dough. Can you let me have some more?'

'I can,' said Meg. 'Sit down.'

She moved about her kitchen, taking down one jar after another, sure and quick in her choices. When she had assembled what she needed and given Kit a paper packet, she offered him a drink.

He hesitated only for a second; he could hardly trust Meg not to poison the queen's ladies and then reject what she prepared for him.

They sat companionably by the hearth, sipping something herbal from pots without handles.

'How is Mistress Pembroke?' Meg asked him. 'You must have been able to talk to her several times, if my powder has worked on her women.'

'It has worked marvellously well, thank you, Mistress Meg. She is in a strange mood, it seems to me, but you must remember that I never met her before she came into the Tower.'

'How strange?'

'Well, you would think she would be always fearful and weeping but she is often merry and makes jests. Even though she is afraid of what the women will tell the constable and through him, the king.'

'She was always quick to change her moods,' said Meg. 'And sometimes said what she shouldn't. I think it was one of the things the king loved about her – that she was sunshine and tempests all in the same moment.'

'How did you meet her?' asked Kit, not sure whether he was being impudent.

Meg sighed and looked sad. 'The poor lady came to me for help in bearing a male child. I did my best for her but it was not to be. I cannot make a miracle.'

'I heard she lost a male child in January,' said Kit. 'After the king was hurt at Greenwich.'

'I heard that too and I feared for her then. She came to me once more a month later and asked for a love potion. She feared she was losing the king's affection.'

Kit thought of the queen slipping through the streets of London in a humble disguise and knocking on the door of Meg's little house, in a desperate attempt to keep the king's love.

'Jane Seymour,' he said quietly.

'Indeed,' said Meg. 'I think she knew then that the king had made up his mind.'

The poet was pacing his room in the Bell Tower when Kit took him his supper, as if he had been walking back and forth all day.

By now the guard was used to Kit waiting while Wyatt ate and drank and let him stay till he could bring the empty basket and platters down.

'What news, Kit?' said Wyatt, starting as always to drink his wine before he bothered with any food.

'I have found out who the lord is and where he lives,' said Kit.

'Good. Don't say it aloud. The Tower walls may have ears. I don't need to know. But how did you find out?'

'I met the boy who runs the secretary's errands,' said Kit.

'And Cromwell knows this lord? Surely he doesn't know what he is planning?'

'I am sure he does not,' said Kit. 'This servant – Will, he's called – thinks that the secretary doesn't much like this lord, even though they seem to share some of the same aims. He showed me the face he pulls when he sends Will to him with a message.'

Kit demonstrated this face to the poet, who laughed.

'Oh Kit, you do me good! My time here in the Tower would have been so much grimmer without you.'

He began to tuck into slices of mutton.

'I have seen that face on the secretary,' said Wyatt. 'I think he has to have dealings with a lot of people he doesn't like or trust.'

'But he and the lord agree on some things,' said Kit. 'And those do not look good for the queen.'

The poet sighed. 'She was most unwise to quarrel with him. He is not only the cleverest man in the kingdom but also the most dangerous.'

'And yet you think he bears no malice towards the little princess?'

'He is not a devil,' said Wyatt. 'Though some people

would disagree. I do not believe he would harm a little girl who can barely walk and talk.'

'I hope not,' said Kit, 'but that doesn't bother the lord or his steward or the ruffians they are going to pay.'

'He had two little girls himself, you know,' said Wyatt.

Kit hadn't known. He knew the secretary had a son, quite a grown-up one, and that he was a widower.

'What happened to them?'

'Died of the same fever that took their mother,' said Wyatt.

He had finished eating and gave Kit his cup to re-fill with wine.

'Life does not deal fairly with us, Kit,' he said and the boy knew the poet meant that he would willingly have lost his own wife rather than Cromwell lose his. Thomas Wyatt did not love his wife.

Had Thomas Cromwell loved his?

'He is not a devil,' Wyatt repeated. 'He loved his wife and daughters and loves his son still. He is a man like the rest of us.'

'And yet you think the queen is here because she quarrelled with him? Not because she did . . . those things she is accused of?'

Thomas Wyatt sighed deeply.

'The quarrel with Cromwell would not have mattered if the king had still loved her, Kit,' he said. 'No one would have dared to move against her.'

Kit quietly packed up the supper basket and knocked on the door to call the guard.

Kit went to visit the ravens after leaving the Bell Tower. It was a fine night and the stars were bright over the city. Most of the birds were asleep but Bran still looked out over the cobbles of the town-within-the-town that was the Tower of London.

'Good evening, Your Majesty,' Kit said to the big black bird, bowing to the one king he could understand.

'Good evening, young Kit,' said the raven. 'Can you not sleep?'

'I promised my father I would check on you all,' said Kit. 'He noticed that Huginn and Muninn looked tired again yesterday.'

'They are in fine fettle,' said Bran. 'We are all willing to do anything we can to help save the little princess.'

'Thank you,' said Kit. 'The trouble is, I still don't know when the attack is going to happen. If I leave it too long, it might be too late to save her.'

Bran prukked softly.

'You are not alone, Kit,' he said. 'You have the birds of the air to help you and Isabel and Alice and even the poet.'

Kit went to bed comforted. There was a small chance that he would succeed but it was true that he wouldn't have to do it on his own. And he could add Mossy Meg and, he thought, Will Rede to the list of his friends.

*

In another part of town the secretary was sitting up late reading through his papers. The trial tomorrow must not bring any surprises.

He yawned and rubbed his tired eyes. His candle burned down. But Cromwell did not think he would get any sleep that night. Tomorrow four men would face judgement and then how many nights would be left for them on this earth? He wondered if he should keep vigil for them and not sleep again until they slept for ever.

His servant brought him fresh candles and hot spiced wine.

Cromwell shuffled the papers on his desk. He knew what a dangerous game he was playing. If it all went well – which was to say badly for the queen and her followers – the king would have a new wife. He would be happy and, what was better, he would be pleased with the secretary who had made it possible.

And if it went badly? In other words, if the queen and the men accused with her were *not* found guilty? It was unthinkable.

Everything depended on tomorrow's trial. If the four men were found guilty, the queen could not be innocent. The outcome of her trial would be certain.

The top piece of paper was another plea from Francis Weston's family, offering huge sums of money for him to go free. The secretary shook his head.

There was a scuffling sound outside his door. In two strides he was across the room with a candle and yanked it open. A sleepy Will Rede fell in.

'Ah, Will,' said Cromwell. 'I thought you were a rat. What are you doing there?'

Will stood, knuckling sleep out of his eyes.

'I was told to wait all night, sir, in case you needed me for messages. They said it was an important night.'

'Well "they" were right,' said Cromwell. 'But you might as well come in and make yourself comfortable.'

He gestured to a chair and poured the boy a cup of spiced wine. 'Take this to warm you. I have no messages for you at the moment but it will be a long night.'

Will curled up in the chair, warming his hands on the cup and inhaling the smell of cinnamon and cloves. 'Thank you, sir.'

'Do you know why it is an important night, Will?' asked Cromwell.

Will shook his head. 'No, sir.'

He thought it safer to be ignorant.

'Tomorrow four men will be tried for treason,' said Cromwell. 'All members of the king's inner circle, except for the musician.'

'That must make the king sad,' said Will. 'To have his friends turn against him.'

'But did they? Or did he turn against them? He *is* sad though, Will. He is full of sadness but for himself more than for the men he believes plotted his death and lay with his wife. He has written his own account of what happened and calls it his True Tragedy. He carries it with him everywhere and reads from it to anyone who will listen.'

'He wouldn't read it to me, sir,' said Will.

'No. Truly, he would not. And I should not have spoken of it, even to you. But we are alone and you will forget it. You will forget anything I say to you tonight, won't you?'

'I can be very forgetful,' said Will.

'Good boy. You will be a politician one day. Will you watch this night with me, Will?'

'I shall try, sir.'

But when the dawn came, the secretary was still sitting grey-faced at his desk and Will Rede was fast asleep in the chair.

10

The Great Axe

A shadow hung over the Tower the next morning. Every soul within the walls knew that today would mark the beginning of the end for the prisoners, from the lowly commoner Mark Smeaton, right up to the queen herself.

Kit snatched a hasty breakfast as his home was in turmoil.

'I have been ordered to accompany the constable to Westminster, Kit,' said the Ravenmaster, as his wife brushed down his uniform. 'They need as many guards as possible for the four accused men. You will have to see to the birds.'

Kit didn't mind that.

'You must remember all that passes and come back to us with the full story,' said Marjorie. 'We shall all be thinking of the trial today.'

They went with the Ravenmaster down to the water gate, where the four accused were being put on a barge, in the charge of Sir William Kingston, the constable.

The lieutenant was there too, with Alice, who exchanged glances with Kit. George Atwood stood nearby, glaring at him.

As soon as the barge left Alice asked her father if she could go with Kit to see the ravens.

'He can bring me to the queen afterwards,' said Alice.

'If you take care the birds do not come close to my daughter with their cruel beaks and talons,' said the lieutenant. 'And then promise to bring her straight away to the queen's lodgings.'

'I will, sir,' said Kit. 'I have to take the bread up to the queen and her waiting women each morning.'

The lieutenant raised an eyebrow, but handed his daughter over to Kit. They walked back together with his mother to the raven cages.

The ravens had waited patiently for their breakfast, knowing it was an unusual day. But they were hungry and snatched the food from Kit's hands.

'They do have terrible beaks and claws,' said Alice. 'But I don't believe they would hurt me. And they would never hurt you, Kit.'

'Only by accident,' said Kit, knowing how many scars he and his father bore on their hands from when the ravens had been too quick and eager for their food.

When they had eaten, the ravens walked up and down and some took short flights, as if their flight feathers had still been trimmed but Kit had stopped doing that to all of them. He wasn't sure when he might need all six of them to go spying for him.

Marjorie hadn't stayed. 'I am going to clean the house from roof to cellar,' she said. 'I need something to keep me busy today.'

Once she had gone, Bran told Kit that he had birds stationed at the lord's house, the secretary's and at Hunsdon.

'And every bird in London is ready to pick up any gossip – we'll know the trial verdict long before your father is back.'

'What is he saying?' asked Alice.

Kit told her only the last bit. He didn't want to alarm her about the princess.

They went back to the green and into the bakery, to collect the queen's bread. Isabel curtseyed briefly to Alice who blushed and bobbed slightly back.

'We are friends, aren't we, Isabel?' she asked. 'All working for the same thing,' she added under her breath.

Isabel cast a look at Kit, standing patiently at Alice's side, and thrust the basket of bread at him.

'Get along with you quickly,' she said. 'You are keeping the queen waiting.'

But it was her ladies who complained about the lateness of their breakfast. The queen stood silently at the window, uninterested in food, while Alice poured the small beer that a servant had brought.

Kit left them and hurried back to the Bell Tower to wait on Thomas Wyatt.

He never complained even though this was the latest he had ever been brought washing water and food in the morning.

'So your father is at the trial, Kit?' he said. 'You must tell me all about it this evening. Though I fear there can be only one outcome for all of the men.'

'Do you know them, sir?' asked Kit, wondering what it must be like to know people who were doomed, probably to a most horrible death.

'I do,' said the poet, crumbling a piece of bread between his fingers. He seemed to have no more appetite than the queen. 'Norris has been the closest thing the king has had to a friend for twenty years or more. Brereton has been with him almost as long.'

'The other two are younger men, I think,' said Kit.

'Weston is only twenty-five,' said Wyatt. 'He was just a page ten years ago. But the king liked to play sports and games with him, so he became a favourite. The musician too, though he is a commoner. He can't be much more than twenty years old, damn him.'

'Why must he be damned, sir?'

'Because if he hadn't confessed to Cromwell, none of the rest of us would have been arrested.'

'But you haven't been charged with anything!' exclaimed Kit, suddenly alarmed that he might have a friend going to such a dreadful trial soon.

'No, and I shan't be,' said Wyatt. 'The secretary has promised my father.'

*

There was no comfort to be had in Kit's home: Marjorie was busy shaking mattresses out of the upper windows. She gave him some coins and sent him to the bakery to buy a pie for his midday meal.

Isabel was taking a few minutes' rest to eat something, sitting on a bench in the corner. Her father grunted when he saw Kit but let him in and served him; Kit was well known enough not to have to wait at the counter.

He took his pie and went to sit next to Isabel and they ate in companionable silence, listening as people came up to the counter and gossiped with Isabel's father.

'No one seems to know anything about the trial,' Kit whispered to Isabel.

'It doesn't stop them talking about it though,' said Isabel. 'Every man here is a juror or judge.'

'Can you put Meg's powder in the queen's bread tomorrow?' asked Kit. 'My father will tell me everything that happened at the trial and I'm sure she'll want to hear about it.'

'Lady Kingston will tell her.'

'But will she tell her the truth?'

Thomas Wagstaffe had never been so glad to come off duty and get back to his home and family. The day's work had turned his stomach.

Nevertheless, he wanted to eat his supper before he told Marjorie and Kit his account. They both watched him eat every mouthful and drink every drop of his ale.

Eventually, he pushed his platter and cup away and stood up from the table.

'Where are you going?' asked his wife.

'To see to the birds.'

'It's all done, Father,' said Kit. 'And I've put them away for the night.'

'So early?'

'I expect he wanted everything done before you came home so you could tell us all about the trial,' said Marjorie.

The Ravenmaster sighed. He had known he must tell this tale and had been framing sentences in his mind all the way home from Westminster on the barge.

'Tell it all from the beginning,' said Marjorie encouragingly.

'Well, I wasn't there three years ago in Westminster when the queen was crowned, but some of the other warders had been,' said Thomas. 'I could hear them muttering about the difference in the hall – no blue and gold carpet and tapestries this time, only tiers of wooden benches, like at an entertainment.'

'Ha!' said Marjorie. 'I expect it was for some. Like bear-baiting.'

'The jurymen filed into court and the accused men knew they were done for. They were all men in Cromwell's pocket or supporters of the Seymour family or of the Lady Mary.'

'Didn't the accused men object to any of them?' asked Marjorie.

'Maybe they weren't allowed to,' said Kit.

'They could have done,' said his father. 'But I think they didn't want to make a fuss. After all, it is still in the king's power to pardon them or at least show mercy over the sentence.'

Kit shuddered.

'And I suppose there is no doubt what that was?' asked Marjorie.

'I thought you wanted me to tell you everything from the beginning?'

Marjorie gave her husband a look and he continued.

'Smeaton was the only one who pleaded guilty,' he said. 'At least to, well, to lying with the queen. But not to treason. Not to plotting the king's death.'

Kit didn't really understand how a musician could plot a king's death. But then he couldn't imagine the queen loving a commoner either. But why had the lute-player admitted to something that hadn't happened?

'Everyone else pleaded not guilty to all charges. But it went on for hours because of all the details and dates given by the Crown prosecutors. And although the men denied everything, the jurors all voted for their guilt.'

It was only what Kit had expected but hearing it made it worse.

'And then the great axe was turned with its blade towards them and the sentence pronounced – the full penalty for treason.'

Kit couldn't stay to hear more; he rushed out and lost his supper behind the nearest bush.

After a while, he stood up and headed for the Bell Tower. The guard was so used to seeing him waiting on the poet that he let him go up, even though he had finished all his duties for the night.

'Kit!' said Wyatt. 'Your father is back? I have heard the verdict but none of the details.'

Kit told him all he could remember of his father's account.

'Do you really think it will happen?' Kit asked when he had run out of information.

'They will certainly die,' said the poet. 'The only question is how. Let us hope the king shows some mercy.'

Marjorie was waiting up for Kit.

'I was worried about you, love,' she said. 'Your father went to see if you were with the birds but he couldn't find you.'

'I went to see the poet,' said Kit. 'I'm all right. It was just . . . thinking about the sentence.'

'It won't be done here,' said Marjorie. 'At Tyburn, your father said.'

'It's not the place that was upsetting me,' said Kit. 'It was the thing itself. How can one man do that to another?'

Marjorie sighed. 'All this business is making you grow up too fast. It is not something that people like us have to fear, though. We don't get tangled up in the affairs of kings and nobles.'

That did not comfort Kit as much as it might have.

After all, he *was* entangled in royal affairs. He could just stop meeting the queen and forget about the plot against the princess; that was what a wise person would do.

But, although he was more frightened than he had ever been in his life, Kit knew he could not stop.

The queen stood like a pillar in the midst of ruins, as her women lay unconscious around her. She was as white as marble. Kit could tell straight away that she had heard news of the trial. Lady Kingston would not have been kind in the telling.

'Kit,' she said. 'You have heard?'

'My father was there and told me.'

'Oh yes, he was there,' said the queen. 'I remember.' She seemed distracted: her clothes were disarrayed and her hair not dressed. It tumbled uncombed down her back.

Alice looked upset. It was her job to help the queen dress and it seemed she hadn't been allowed to do it today.

'They are all to die – horribly,' said the queen. 'You know what this means?'

'We are all praying for the king's mercy,' said Kit.

'Mercy? Do you know what Kingston said to me? He said that the king's poorest subject had justice. The justice of the lion, Kit, and the mercy of the cat towards the mouse.'

Kit had not seen the queen in this mood before. There was none of the laughter and gaiety of their previous meetings, even if her merriment had always tottered on the edge of hysteria. This morning she was grave and sober. Kit wondered if she were thinking about the cruel punishment of the man who claimed he had been her lover and the three who had denied it.

'Poor foolish Mark Smeaton,' she said now. 'His young flesh to be so tortured. And all for a vain boast that turned into a confession. You know what their sentence means for me?'

She walked among the bodies of her women like the survivor of a massacre. But that was exactly what she was not.

'I hate to know that you have heard these wicked things said of me, my knight. But you are not too young to know that if a man has been found guilty of adultery then the woman must also be guilty. And if one is convicted of plotting the king's death with the queen then that queen must also have plotted it.

'I am dead, Kit. I know you see me walking and talking but I am a ghost in advance of my own death. I cannot be saved.'

'Your Grace, let me help you with your hair and clothes,' said Alice, as gently as she could. 'You will feel better.'

'Will I?' said the queen. 'Is there any reason to be clean and neat? To feed this worthless body? Is it only so that I can make a better corpse?'

'The reason is that you are the queen,' said Kit. 'You must *be* the queen till the end of your days however many they may be. You cannot have people say that you let the king win.'

The queen stood up and straightened her shoulders.

'You are right,' she said. 'I was always good at the game of being a court lady – until the very end when I made such terrible mistakes. I shall be a court lady – and a queen – till the end. Alice, please do help me to make a better figure. Kit, please send to Hunsdon again. The only thing that will allow me to bear it like a queen is if you keep reassuring me that my daughter is safe.'

And Kit ran down the stairs more determined than ever to save the princess. It was the only thing he could do for the queen and he would do it if it cost him his life.

11

As the Boy Walks

He cannoned straight into George at the foot of the stairs, who glared at him.

'What are you doing in the queen's apartments?' he said.

Kit showed him the basket he was carrying.

'I take up the women's bread every morning,' he said. 'And I forgot to fetch back the basket.'

George frowned but although he looked fierce there was nothing he could really fault Kit for.

'Are you waiting for Alice?' asked Kit.

'Yes. Not that it's any of your business. I told you before – Alice Walsingham isn't for the likes of you. And nor is Isabel, come to that. I don't know why you waste your time mooning over them.'

'I suppose they are both in love with you, George?' said Kit, twisting past him. 'Why don't you go and look after your bear? They are as likely to fall in love with that as with a great loon like you.'

And he ran anyway before George could grab him.

Panting, he came to where the ravens were walking up and down on the grass near their cages.

'Ah, Kit!' said Bran, as soon as he saw him. 'There is news. Chaffinches from the city and doves from Hunsdon.'

Kit threw himself down on the grass. 'Tell me.'

'I'm afraid it is rather worrying,' said Bran. 'It took a long time to understand the finches but I think what they have found out is that the kidnap of the princess will happen the same day that the queen is executed.'

'What!' Kit sat upright. 'But the queen hasn't even been tried yet! Not till Monday. How can they know when that . . . when that thing will happen?'

'They are only finches, Kit, not lawyers or statesmen. But the lord certainly believes that the queen will die. And if the plot is already in place, it will not be difficult to carry it out as soon as the day of her death is announced.'

'I suppose that makes sense. If that day comes then all attention will be on the Tower. It would be easier for them to capture the princess.'

He still couldn't bring himself to believe that the lord's plan was to kill the little girl.

'What about Hunsdon?' he asked at last.

'That is hard to understand, too,' said Bran. 'The doves say that Elizabeth – "the princess with the tawny feathers" was what they actually said – is well but they seemed to have picked up that she is not closely watched any more. I asked them to count the guards and the number of attendants but they aren't very good at numbers. We have been trying to work something out with seeds.'

'Then we need to send ravens again,' said Kit.

'Let me go with Blodwen,' said Bran. 'The doves can show the way. And Huginn and Muninn have done too many long flights.'

'How are your feathers feeling?' asked Kit.

In answer the King Raven spread his impressive black wings to their full extent, threw back his head and cawed his most raucous cry.

In spite of all his worries, Kit had to smile.

'Go, then,' he said. 'I would feel better if I had news from ravens.'

He went back home for the midday meal and found his parents in a sombre mood.

'What has happened?' he asked.

'It's only a rumour,' said his father. 'But the word is going round that the king has ordered a swordsman from Calais and he is already on his way.'

'To execute the men?' asked Kit. 'Does that mean their sentence has changed?'

Thomas and Marjorie exchanged looks.

'Kit, I know you are very attached to the queen,' said Marjorie, 'but it's time you accepted what is going to happen to her. The French executioner is for her.'

'But she hasn't been tried yet!' said Kit. His mouth felt so dry with fear he could hardly get the words out.

'The king,' said his father, then stopped and looked

out the window to check there was no one else nearby. 'The king is the ultimate power in the land, higher than any court of law. At least, that's what he believes. If he has decided to re-marry, then the queen's life will be the price.'

'But why doesn't he just divorce her, like the last queen?' asked Kit. He couldn't understand anyone being this cold-blooded towards the wife he had once loved. 'I know she would be willing to go into a convent – she told Lady Kingston so.'

Thomas sighed. 'I can't answer that, Kit. But times have changed. Maybe the king thinks he cannot go through all that opposition and hostility again.'

'Do you think he really believes his wife committed treason and loved all those other men?' Kit was close to tears.

'I'm sure he does believe it now,' said Marjorie quietly, 'even if it is not true. He has to believe it if he is to go through with his plan.'

'Then why didn't he do that with Queen Katherine?' asked Kit. 'If he made all this up, or the secretary did, couldn't they have done that last time? It would have been easier than everything you have told me about the business with the Pope.'

'No one would have believed it of good, plain Queen Katherine,' said Marjorie.

And there it was.

Kit was sure that the queen was innocent but he had to admit that people had been very ready to believe the worst of her. She was not popular and she was – what had she said? – 'good at the game of being a court lady'.

She had been merry and flirtatious even with a humble boy of the Tower – even when the great axe was hanging over her. Or the French sword. She hadn't done those things she was accused of but people could imagine that she had and *that* was what was going to kill her.

Kit's heart felt too big for his chest. He had lost his appetite. Everything was happening so quickly. He had to decide what to do about the plot against the Princess Elizabeth.

Wandering aimlessly round the only place he could remember as his home, he found himself by the Lion Tower. The smell brought him back to his senses. Kit tried to avoid the menagerie as much as possible. Unlike the ravens, these animals were never allowed out of their cages and it made him sad.

But today he felt drawn to see the bear.

Checking carefully that George was nowhere in sight, Kit went into the enclosed space that stank of blood and manure and the smell of animal fear. A few members of the public were paying to see the animals but Kit was waved through; everyone knew he was a child of the Tower.

He passed the two lions and the lonely leopard, who paced back and forth like a sleepwalker. It reminded Kit of the poet.

The bear was enormous.

It lay sprawled on the stone floor, its huge shaggy

head resting on its paws. It didn't look too menacing at the moment but Kit could imagine what it would be like if it stood up on its back legs. And he could see scars on its snout where he guessed it had been prodded with a staff to make it roar and look terrifying.

He wondered if anywhere in the world there was a boy who could speak Bear and if there were, what he would hear from this prisoner. Unlike the other prisoners in the Tower, this one would never go free.

The bear opened one yellow eye and looked at Kit.

'I wish I could help you,' whispered Kit. 'But there are too many things I can't do anything about.'

He left the menagerie with a heavy heart and soon found himself by the main gate.

'Kit!' called a cheery voice, startling him out of his lethargy. 'I was coming to find you.'

Will Rede took off his cap and his hair blazed like a fire Kit could warm his hands on.

Immediately he felt better. 'Will! It's good to see you.'

'Friend of yours?' asked the warder on the gate.

'Yes,' said Kit and felt it to be true. 'Come and meet my family. And the ravens.'

As the two boys walked through the cobbled streets, Kit realised that something had changed in the atmosphere. After the terrible tension of yesterday, it was as if all the inhabitants of this fortress had relaxed.

Well, all except the men doomed to die, I suppose, thought Kit.

He realised that the change in the air was not relief but acceptance. The first storm had broken and ordinary people were just getting on with their lives, trying not to get wet.

'You don't have to work for the secretary today?' asked Kit.

'I have a few hours free,' said Will. 'I thought I could take you to the lord's house, so that you could find your way there again if you needed to.'

'I'll ask my father if I can go out for a few hours,' said Kit. He would have to wait for the evening to hear from Bran and Blodwen and going out with Will would fill those anxious hours.

Marjorie was very taken with Will and pleased that Kit had somehow found a friend outside the Tower. She had been worried about how his life was too full of thoughts of a doomed queen and an imprisoned poet.

'You don't have to do chores this afternoon,' she said. 'It will do you good to get away from the Tower, as long as you are back in time for your duties with the birds. But go and see your father first.'

She gave them both a jam tart and by the time they found the Ravenmaster there was nothing left but crumbs.

Will was impressed by the ravens he saw, who were Thomas and Bess. They were strutting round Thomas Wagstaffe's feet but clattered their beaks when they saw Kit.

'This is Will, Father,' said Kit. 'He works for the secretary but he is not here on business.'

The Ravenmaster shook Will's hand.

'They are the biggest birds I have ever seen,' Will said, then jumped back in fright.

Kit laughed. 'It's all right,' he said. 'They've spotted the crumbs on your jerkin.'

The boys stood very still while the ravens cleared up the last of the tarts.

'Good,' said Wagstaffe. 'You didn't move. That's braver than most people are.'

'Mother said it was all right for me to go out for an hour or two with Will,' said Kit. 'I'll be back in time to feed the birds.'

'Qu'aark,' said Bess.

'The ravens I mean,' said Kit.

His father was happy for the boys to go somewhere together so they were soon outside the golden walls of the Tower.

'They're nice, your parents,' said Will. 'I've got none myself but if I had, I'd like them to be like yours.'

'You're an orphan?' said Kit.

'Yes. It's all right. I never knew them. The secretary took me into his household when I was a littl'un. He's been good to me – a bit like a father. He makes sure everyone in his household is well fed and has warm clothes.'

'I'm an orphan too,' said Kit. 'The man I call "Father" now rescued me from a plague cart when my parents died. It was so long ago that I can't remember my first mother and father properly. My new ones are all the family I've got.'

He didn't mention that he sometimes dreamed about the baker and his wife.

The two boys looked at each other and felt a new bond had formed between them.

'I have some news,' said Will. 'My master got a message from Whitehall. The queen's household is being broken up tomorrow.'

Kit shivered. He remembered the queen saying, 'I am dead, Kit.'

'And I have heard that the king has sent for a swordsman from Calais,' he said.

Will nodded. 'I heard that too. I didn't want to say. I know you think the queen shouldn't die.'

They walked through the streets with Kit now taking note of where he was going. It took longer but was much easier to remember, because Will was leading him not as the crow – or raven – flies, but as a boy might again find his way walking from the Tower to the lord's residence.

Kit knew the name of the street now as well as the name of the lord but he was somehow superstitious about saying it aloud.

The two boys went to the back of the house and quickly Will pushed Kit back round the corner, out of sight.

'What is it?'

'Shh! It's the steward. He's coming out.'

Kit had never seen the lord's steward and would

have missed his chance to follow him if he hadn't been with Will.

The boys tagged along after the tall figure, following him at a distance through a maze of streets until they were in a poorer part of town. Then the steward ducked into a tavern, first looking left and right along the street and tying a mask over his face, but taking no notice of two ordinary boys.

'Now what can we do?' said Kit. 'We will look out of place in a tavern.'

'We can pretend we have been sent for a jug of ale by our master,' said Will, 'if anyone asks.'

'What, both of us?'

'Have you a better plan?'

Kit didn't but they needn't have worried. The tavern was very full and no one took any notice of them. Kit was beginning to realise just how invisible a sixteen-year-old boy – or even two – could be in a big city. Children and young people were a minority in the Tower but the streets of London were full of them.

They pushed their way through the crowd until they saw the steward. He was buying ale for three very rough-looking men and Kit knew immediately who they were.

'That's them,' he whispered. 'The three the lord is paying to kidnap the princess – or worse.'

He heard one of the rough men call the steward 'Burford'.

'That's not his name,' whispered Will. 'I've taken messages to him. He's called . . .'

But Kit put his hand over his friend's mouth.

'Don't say it,' he said. 'He's going by "Arthur Burford" here. I remember the birds told Bran.'

Will looked at Kit oddly; he didn't know the full story yet of how his new friend got his information.

They inched closer.

The men were talking about the trial but there was nothing incriminating in that – most of London was talking about it.

'So, why do we need to wait?' asked one of them. 'If the men are bound for execution, then she is too.'

The steward looked round nervously and lowered his voice.

'We must wait until she is condemned too and a date fixed for the execution,' he said. 'The king is very changeable. He might overturn everything. But not once the court has passed sentence. And her trial is on Monday – there is not long to wait.'

'Do you want us to stay in London till we hear from you?' asked another of the ruffians.

'No,' said the steward. 'I want you to move to Hunsdon now and spy out the land. Take a room in the village – in the inn called the Green Man – and I'll send word to you when it is safe to move.'

He passed them a bag that Kit could see was heavy with money.

The men grinned as their leader hefted the bag.

'As good as done,' he said. 'Trust us – her days are numbered.'

12

No Love Lost

Kit was back at the Tower in good time for Bran and Blodwen's return. He was worried that his father was getting suspicious about the ravens' ever-increasing disappearances.

And the two birds did look a bit dishevelled, especially Blodwen.

'That was the longest flight I've done since they caught me in Wales,' she said. Bran groomed her head feathers for her.

'You got to Hunsdon all right?' asked Kit. 'And saw the little princess?'

'We did,' said Bran. 'And I think all your fears are justified. She does not have enough attendants or guards.'

'What should we do?' asked Kit. 'How can I get word to them? Shall I tell someone official?'

'I think you should tell someone,' said Bran. 'But not an official – not yet. I think you should tell the Ravenmaster.'

Kit's heart sank. He had thought before about telling his parents what he was doing but he didn't know if they would forbid him from carrying on. And if they did, the princess would be doomed.

'Why not do it now?' cawed Blodwen.

Kit saw his father coming towards them.

'They don't look good, do they?' he said to Kit. 'I wonder if there is a bird illness going around? I've been worried about Hugh and Moony recently.'

'It's not an illness,' said Kit. 'I'm afraid it's my fault.'

Thomas Wagstaffe gave him a keen look. 'Do you want to tell me what you mean?'

'Well, you know that I can understand what the ravens are saying and that they can understand me?'

'Yes. It's something I try not to think about much because it is too strange. But if it's affecting the well-being of the birds, then you do need to tell me.'

Fifteen minutes later, the Ravenmaster sat down on a bench and mopped his brow with a handkerchief.

'And this has been going on for weeks?' he asked at last. 'The not trimming of flight feathers and sending the birds out to spy and finding out a plot about the princess?'

'Yes,' said Kit.

'And you've been poisoning loaves and talking to the queen and the poet has been sending her messages?'

'I told you,' said Kit.

'Then you have been dabbling in matters you don't understand and putting us all in peril!' said his father. 'Have you any idea how dangerous this all is?'

'I think so,' said Kit. 'But not as dangerous as it is for the princess. What else could I do once I knew what that lord was planning?'

Kit's father considered this. 'I suppose that's true,' he said.

It gave Kit a small ray of hope. His father was a kind man. Hadn't he saved Kit from certain death? And wouldn't he do the same for a little girl whose mother was doomed to die?

'But this is too big for us, Kit,' said the Ravenmaster. 'We must tell someone else – someone with more power.'

'That's what the poet thinks,' said Kit. 'But can we try to warn the people at Hunsdon ourselves first?'

'How would we do that?' said his father. 'I need to talk to your mother and we need to sleep on it. This is too important to decide while we are tired and taken by surprise.'

'We can't wait too long though,' said Kit. 'The queen's trial is the day after tomorrow.'

But he went to bed with a lighter heart than he had felt for days. Marjorie had been just as worried as his father but she hadn't said that Kit must stop what he had been doing. It felt good to have his parents on his side.

The secretary slept little that night, although it had been a long day. The trial of the four men had gone as planned but now he was trying to get their sentences reduced to the more merciful one of beheading. It shouldn't be too hard to accomplish for the three gentlemen but Mark Smeaton was a bigger problem.

As a commoner convicted of treason he should have been subject to the full rigour of the gruesome penalty. But the secretary had promised him mercy if he confessed everything. And though Cromwell was aware that the musician had thought this meant saving his life, that had never been part of the plan.

Still, he was determined to give the foolish young man a clean and painless death.

'Is it ever painless?' he wondered aloud, feeling his own thick neck and thinking about an axe trying to slice through it.

He had forgotten that Will Rede was in his room, waiting for instructions. Two almost sleepless nights in a row had fogged the secretary's brain.

'What is it, Master?' asked Will.

'Nothing, boy, nothing,' said Cromwell. 'I was thinking aloud. About execution. Nothing you need ever worry about, I'm sure.'

There was a knock at the door and another messenger brought in a letter for the secretary. He had several boys in his household to carry out such errands and there was a friendly rivalry among them.

'Ah, bad news,' he said when he had sent the other messenger away and opened the letter. 'Will, I must write a message for you to take to the king. Can you do that?'

'At the palace, sir? I can do that.'

'Wait while I write it. This is going to be difficult.' Cromwell sighed.

'Can I fetch you something to eat while I wait?' asked Will.

'You are a good-hearted boy,' said his master. 'Yes, thank you. Maybe some bread and ale will clear my head a little. The king is not going to be happy to receive my letter.'

'Shall I wait for a reply?' asked Will.

'Yes, you had better.'

The boy ran quickly to the kitchen and brought back a plate and cup for the secretary, by which time he was folding up a letter and melting wax on to it to seal it.

'Wait a bit while I have my breakfast, Will,' he said. 'I might change my mind.'

'About what you need to say?' asked Will.

'About how I am to say it,' said Cromwell. 'How is your reading and writing coming on, by the way?'

'I am doing quite well, sir,' said Will. He had been having lessons for some time but they had to be fitted in round his tasks. Still, Cromwell was a good master and wanted his cleverer boys to learn skills that would bring them better work in time.

'I wish you could write this one for me,' said the secretary.

'It is a hard letter, sir?'

'It is, Will. I have to tell a powerful man, one used to having his own way, that I cannot solve his problem in the way he wants.'

'And he will be angry with you?'

'A little,' said the secretary, smiling. 'But I have learned how to handle this particular lion. If I can't bring him a haunch of venison I must hide half a cow behind my back, ready to offer him as soon as the absence of venison has been seen.'

'Then I hope you never run out of meat, sir,' said Will.

The secretary laughed full-throatedly.

'I told you that you should be a politician one day, Will,' he said, wiping his eyes. 'And I was right. Thank you for making me laugh during these dark days.'

Will knew it was the king who would have to be fed different meat. He wondered if it was in the letter he was going to carry to the palace. Cromwell had let fall the letter he had been reading so Will picked it up and handed it back to him. His sharp eyes spotted that the broken seal bore the impression of a lion too. But just two, not six, like the king's seal.

Over the ravens' breakfast, Thomas Wagstaffe told Kit what he had decided. Kit felt sorry for his father, seeing how tired his eyes looked, as if he and Kit's mother had been awake most of the night talking. And it was all Kit's fault for not just staying a Ravenmaster's boy.

'We think – your mother and I,' said the Ravenmaster, 'that if you have a plan for some way to get the news of your fears to Hunsdon, then we should let you have one attempt.'

Kit opened his mouth to speak but his father held up a hand.

'Wait. If that one attempt fails, we must go to the authorities with all your information, even if it puts us all in danger. The safety of the princess is paramount.'

'What authorities?' asked Kit, even though he had no plan in mind.

'Well, initially the constable, I suppose,' said his father. 'But, ultimately, the king.'

'And what if the king already knows?' said Kit.

It had been said now – the thing that had weighed on his mind for so long. His father looked as horrified as Kit felt.

'You mean that the king might be behind a plot to murder his own daughter?'

'Well,' said Kit, lowering his voice, 'people are saying he is behind the plot to murder his wife.'

The Ravenmaster was stunned; he couldn't fault Kit's logic.

'But his own child,' he protested softly.

'You know how Princess Mary was reduced to Lady Mary and has to wait on her half-sister?' said Kit. 'Perhaps there would be a worse outcome for the little princess if the king had a new queen and more princes and princesses.'

'Kit, what you say troubles me greatly. I have heard that some of the king's worst advisers have led him to say he should have disposed more thoroughly of the old queen and the old princess before he married his new queen. Could it be that this bad counsel has been poured into his ears again?'

'You see why it is difficult?' said Kit. 'And you still agree we must save the princess?'

'Of course, but now I need to know your plans,' said his father.

And that was where all Kit's ideas came to a halt.

'If only someone at Hunsdon could speak Raven!' he said to the poet, as he took him his breakfast and told him all that had happened.

'Wait!' said Wyatt. 'We are making this too complicated. There is an easier way to use your ravens.'

Kit was very ready to hear a solution that didn't involve the poet's original idea for foiling the kidnap.

'Could your birds carry a message tied to a leg and deliver it to the right person?'

Kit thought about it. 'They could certainly carry such a message to Hunsdon,' he said, beginning to feel excited. 'But how would they know the right person to deliver it to?'

The poet discarded his food and resumed his pacing. Kit wondered if after Thomas Wyatt's captivity there would be a groove worn in the floor of the upper cell at the Bell Tower.

'I know the princess's attendants,' he was saying. 'There is Lady Bryan, and Sir John Shelton's wife, the Lady Anne, also attended on Lady Mary so she might have gone with her to Hunsdon.'

'Anne Shelton?' asked Kit. 'One of the queen's ladies is called that.'

Thomas Wyatt smacked his forehead. 'Of course! Lady Anne is the queen's aunt. She cannot be looking after the princess in Hertfordshire, as she is here in the Tower, doubtless telling the constable everything the queen says.'

'There seems to be no love lost between them,' said Kit.

'They used to be very close,' said the poet, 'when Anne Shelton was looking after the prin— the Lady Mary.'

He looked grim.

'She was not kind to Mary, Kit,' he said and Kit didn't dare ask which Anne had been unkind to the former princess.

'My father told me that the king was advised he should have got rid of the Lady Mary and her mother, by foul means,' he said.

'There is certainly such talk at court,' said Wyatt. 'In fact the rumour was that it was the queen herself who wished it. And that is where the worse rumour sprang from – that she had the old queen poisoned and was planning to do the same to her daughter Mary.'

'But you don't believe that, sir?'

'Of course not! Anne can be devious and she knows how to get men to do her will but she is not a murderess.'

Kit wondered if he should remind the poet of the queen's friendship with a witch who knew how to make powerful potions. But he didn't, because he didn't want to believe the queen was a murderess either.

'So we know that Lady Anne Shelton is not at Hunsdon,' he said instead. 'What about this Lady Bryan?' He remembered that the queen had mentioned her.

'Margaret Bryan is the woman the king most trusts to raise his children,' said Wyatt. 'He gave Mary into her care and she now looks after the Princess Elizabeth.'

'Do you know what she looks like?' asked Kit. 'Perhaps the ravens could take the message to her?'

'I do,' said the poet, struggling to remember. 'I will describe her to you and you must translate it for the ravens. It is certainly worth the attempt.'

Will had loitered at the palace, waiting for the king's reply. Lowly messengers like himself did not enter the Presence Chamber. He had handed over Cromwell's letter to a grand footman dressed in the king's livery and was now sitting in a small lodge at the palace gates, eating a pasty and drinking a cup of small beer.

The guard on the gate was on duty so couldn't talk but the under-footman who had brought Will his refreshment was in a chatty mood. Will had met this one before when he had brought messages to the palace from the secretary and he knew that this royal servant – John by name – was a fount of information about the nobility.

'John,' he asked now. 'Who else has lions passant and guardant on his coat of arms, besides the king?'

'What colour?' asked John immediately.

'I don't know. I saw it impressed on a wax seal only.'

'How many?'

'Two – one in the upper left quarter and one in the lower right,' said Will.

'Ah,' said the under-footman. 'Northumberland. The Earl.'

'And who is that?'

'Henry Percy,' said John. 'The one they say was betrothed to the queen.'

Then he clapped his hand to his mouth. 'Forget I said that!'

'That's all right,' said Will. 'It's forgotten – but thank you!'

But he did not forget it; he stored it up to tell his new friend Kit that his master, the secretary, had received a letter from Henry Percy, Earl of Northumberland, who might once have been betrothed to the queen.

And that the secretary had written to the king because Henry Percy had not provided the answer the king wanted – the haunch of venison that the Lion of England desired to eat.

13

Warnings

It was Sunday and Kit attended Mass at the Chapel of Saint Peter-in-Chains with his parents. He had already fed the ravens and talked to Bran about taking a written message to Hunsdon.

The service was what he needed to calm his mind and strengthen his resolve. Afterwards he left his parents outside and went straight to see the poet.

'We're going to send the message today,' Kit told him. 'Bran will go with Huginn. He thinks Blodwen is too tired.'

'Two of your best ravens,' said the poet. 'It should be enough.'

'But even if they find Lady Bryan, what can she do?' asked Kit. 'Can she take the princess away from Hunsdon without the king's permission?'

'We must leave that to her. If she believes the news, she will act. Of that I am sure.'

'Just as long as she can keep the princess safe till after the queen's death. Do you think it will be enough?'

'That is when we will find out if the king knows anything of the plot,' said Wyatt. 'Once his vengeance and pride has shed enough blood, perhaps – even if he was behind it – he will relent. If not, then those of us who are free must try to get her across the Channel and into France.'

'You trust you will be free?' said Kit.

'I surely hope so. Now, let me help you write the message.'

Will had no messages to carry for the secretary that Sunday morning, so after he had been to church, he went back to the Tower to tell Kit about his errand to the king. Will found him on the green outside the queen's lodgings.

'Is it safe to talk?' he asked.

Kit looked round quickly but saw no eavesdroppers.

'What is it – has something happened?'

'Only that my master has tried and failed to do something that the king wants and he is now trying another way. He had a letter from the Earl of Northumberland and it contained bad news.'

'I know nothing of Northumberland,' said Kit. 'What has he to do with anything?'

'All I know is that he was once betrothed to the queen.'

Another one, thought Kit.

'I will ask the poet what it might mean,' he said. 'We are sending a message to Hunsdon today.'

'There's something else,' said Will. 'I took a message back to my master from the king. He read the letter and said, "So, Queen Jane then." Then he seemed to remember I was there and said, "He is moving her to Chelsea." I asked him if he had found another piece of meat he was going to give the king.'

'Piece of meat?' said Kit.

'It was just something he was talking about to me,' said Will. 'He said the king was like a lion.'

'He isn't the only one to say that,' said Kit. 'I wonder if that's what Jane Seymour thinks?'

'I would not like to be married to a lion,' said Will. 'Unless I was a lioness, I suppose.'

'I think this queen used to be a lioness,' said Kit. 'But now she's more like the lion's prey.'

'Did you speak to her today?'

'No. I am unable to tell her anything good about the princess so we haven't put sleeping powder in the loaves today.'

'And tomorrow is her trial.'

'The men are to be executed on Wednesday,' said Kit. 'Surely they wouldn't kill the queen before them? We think Thursday is the earliest it could happen.'

'Less than a week to live!' said Will. 'What must that feel like?'

'I think they are supposed to think only of their souls, but I couldn't do it.'

'Nor me.'

'Come,' said Kit. 'Let me take you to the bakery and to meet my friend Isabel.'

*

Isabel was flushed and hot from the ovens; even on a Sunday the bread had to be made and all the inhabitants of the Tower fed.

'Back again?' she said to Kit. 'You've already done your duty as baker's boy to the queen.'

'This is my friend, Will,' said Kit. 'He works for the secretary.'

'Ah, yes,' said Isabel. 'Kit has told me about you. Pleased to meet you.'

'And I to meet you, Mistress Isabel,' said Will, making a grand bow.

'I like your friend, Kit – he has the manners of a gentleman.'

Kit wondered if he should bow to her the next time he saw her.

'You have flour on your nose, Isabel,' he said, even though she hadn't.

'You be glad this counter is between us or I would box your ears,' she said, when she had put her hand to her nose and checked.

A savoury aroma rose from the pan, where the meat was bubbling away for a batch of pies, and made the boys' stomachs rumble.

'Have you heard any news this morning?' asked Kit, ducking further away. 'I have told Will that you know all the gossip here.'

Isabel was instantly serious. 'One small piece of good news,' she said. 'There is a rumour that the king will be merciful to the men. But you should know this, Will – what is being said at the secretary's house?'

'I know he was trying for that,' said Will. 'It was a case of catching the king in a good mood and getting him to change the sentence.'

'It's only that, then?' asked Kit. His hopes had risen unreasonably. 'It is not that he will pardon them altogether?'

Isabel and Will turned almost identical looks on him and Will put a hand on his shoulder.

'There is no "only" about the change of penalty,' he said. 'If it is true, I promise you that all four men will be almost as relieved as if they *had* been pardoned.'

Bran and Huginn came back from Hunsdon looking very bedraggled and Kit was glad that at least this time his father knew the reason. They had a long tale to tell and none of it good. But Kit had seen straight away that the messages tied to the birds' legs had gone.

Kit had to wait till they had been groomed by the other ravens and had a long drink and eaten some blood-soaked crusts.

'Are you refreshed enough to tell us what happened now?' said Kit, after a patient wait. His father was standing by to hear the translation of what the ravens had to say.

'We found the woman you described,' said Bran. 'The old one with the grey feathers and long beak.'

'She was with the little princess,' said Huginn.

'So we tapped at the window with our beaks,' said Bran. 'But that seemed to frighten her.'

Kit cursed himself for not realising the flaw in this plan.

Ravens were regarded as birds of ill omen. It wasn't surprising that someone would react with fear to see two huge black birds tapping at the window.

'She didn't open the casement,' said Huginn. 'Instead she hurried out of the room, leaving the small person on her own.'

'Then we saw men on the ground below, throwing sticks and stones up at us,' said Bran. He ruffled all his back plumage up and gave out a loud croak. Clearly this had been an experience that had offended and alarmed him.

'What did you do?' asked Kit.

'We flew higher up, on to the roof,' said Huginn.

'But although we were out of danger,' said Bran, 'we were no closer to delivering your message. We flew round the house a few times.'

'Then the little princess crawled up to the window below,' Bran continued. 'She couldn't open it by herself, but the woman came back and saw what she was doing. "Bird" said the little one. The woman lifted her down from the window.'

'I thought I would try again,' said Huginn. 'So I flew on to the sill and tried to show the woman what I had tied to my leg.'

'She looked then, properly,' said Bran. 'And she seemed to understand.'

'Then what went wrong?' asked Kit.

'It started to rain,' said Huginn. 'We don't mind rain but we didn't understand what this would mean for the messages.'

'It took the woman so long to trust us and open the window and untie the papers,' said Bran.

'She seemed really scared,' said Huginn, clacking his huge beak and looking absurdly offended at being thought in any way dangerous.

'And by then the messages were unreadable?' asked Kit.

He could see it all so clearly it was as if he had been looking through the ravens' eyes. The black ink that he had used to spell out the warning of danger to the princess all streaming down the paper in rivulets to make one illegible mess.

'The woman raised her hands in despair,' said Bran 'and there was nothing we could do except make the long flight home.'

'So that is our one chance gone,' said the Ravenmaster when Kit had finished translating all this.

Kit could not remember ever feeling so dejected. With a heavy heart he went to take the poet an early supper and tell him that their plan had failed.

Thomas Wyatt was not too cast down by Kit's news. He still had his idea for how to save the princess, even though Kit really didn't want to try it.

But the poet was very interested in the news about the Earl of Northumberland's letter.

'Harry Percy?' he said. 'Yes, I remember him well. When the king wanted to marry Anne, he put a lot of pressure on Percy to swear that they had never been properly betrothed – just a little in love like childhood sweethearts – and that it was all in the past.'

'What would it have meant if they *had* been properly betrothed?' asked Kit.

'That Anne Boleyn had a legal attachment and was not free to marry the king, even if he had been free to marry her. And so he could have their marriage declared void.'

'But that was all ages ago,' said Kit. 'Why would Northumberland be writing to the secretary now?'

'You said that your friend told you Cromwell was disappointed with the letter? That he said the king would be a lion deprived of his food?'

'Yes,' said Kit. 'But that he could offer him some other meat. What does it mean?'

The poet paced like the Tower's lone leopard.

'I think it means that the king has asked his secretary to get him divorced again,' he said. 'So he was trying to persuade Percy to take back what he had said before – the last time the king wanted a divorce!'

'But Percy said no?' said Kit.

'So it seems.'

'So what is the "other meat" that the secretary is going to get for the king?'

'I don't know, Kit,' said Wyatt. 'But if anyone can find a possible way, it is Cromwell. He is a very clever man.'

'But if the king is trying to find a way to divorce the queen, then he won't need to kill her!' said Kit. 'He is considering being merciful to the men. Maybe he will be even more merciful to Queen Anne?'

'Maybe, Kit,' said the poet. 'But I would not set your heart on that belief. We must soon try another way to save the princess. We can wait only one more day.'

'For tomorrow's trial?' asked Kit.

He wished that tomorrow would never come. If it had been bad in the Tower during the day of the four men's trial, what on earth would the trial of the queen and her brother be like?

After eating very little of his supper, Kit asked his parents' leave to go out again.

But he didn't just go to visit the ravens; he walked past the menagerie, where he could hear the beasts growling and grumbling, and went right outside the Tower gate.

'Don't be too late coming back, Kit,' said the warden on guard duty. 'I'll open the little postern for you but be back soon.'

Kit wasn't the only person outside the Tower. News that the trial would be held there the next day had spread and there was quite a crowd of people already gathering to talk about the outcome.

Kit walked down to the river's edge. The tide was high and he could see into the boats large and small that were even at this late hour busily travelling the great highway of the Thames.

A wherry pulled into the Tower jetty and a tall, broad-shouldered man stepped out. He wore a thick cloak, even though it was a mild night, and had a velvet hat pulled well down over his face. The wherryman didn't get out on to the jetty.

'Boy!' called the man on the bank.

Kit looked behind him but there was no one else; he went closer to the water.

'You live in the Tower, I think?' said the man.

Kit wondered how he knew.

'I do,' he said.

'What are the people there saying about tomorrow?' asked the man. 'About the queen?'

'I can't say what everyone is saying,' answered Kit, 'but for myself I am sorry for her and think it a great shame if she should lose her life.'

'Ha! Do you? And do you feel sorry for the king too?' asked the man.

'A little,' said Kit. 'But not *as* sorry, for his life is not in danger and people say the king will soon have a new wife.'

'And the queen – if her trial goes against her – will have a new life, won't she?'

'In Heaven, you mean, sir? But she won't have her little daughter with her, will she?'

The man started. 'No, not for a long time, I hope.'

He tossed Kit a coin and stepped back into the wherry. 'To Chelsea,' he said to the boatman.

And as he settled down and drew his cloak around

him, Kit recognised his boots. He had seen them before, the day Blodwen had been brought to the Tower.

Kit looked at the coin in his hand. It was a gold sovereign. If the man was who he thought, then the little princess could still be saved.

14

Trial of a Queen

The next morning Kit thought he must have dreamed his encounter with the cloaked man. But he found the gold coin under his pillow.

He twisted it in a piece of cloth and hid it in his jerkin, his mind in a whirl. If he was right about the man he had seen, then the king was *not* behind any plot to kill his daughter Elizabeth – or even aware of such a plot. That meant the lord was acting on his own. Unless Thomas Cromwell was involved.

With his brain treading in such circles, Kit could not face seeing the queen on the morning of her trial. He asked Isabel to take up the bread and said he would stand in for her in the bakery.

She wasn't long in returning but there was already a disgruntled queue forming. Once Isabel had sorted out what they all wanted, she whispered to Kit.

'She was very disappointed not to see you and made

me promise that you would come to her tomorrow, whatever happens today.'

'So you should put powder in the queen's loaves tomorrow. How did she seem?'

'Calm and sorrowful,' said Isabel.

'I have let her down,' said Kit. 'Her Raven Knight! I am as much use as a Squire of Sparrows.'

'Don't feel guilty,' said Isabel. 'There is more you can do yet, isn't there?'

Kit nodded, too miserable to talk.

'Are you going to the trial?' asked Isabel.

'I will try to get in at the back,' said Kit. 'My father will be on duty.'

The biggest trial ever held at the Tower was going to be heard in the King's Hall, with stands built for two thousand people. There had never been a spectacle like it: a queen and her brother on trial for treason against the king! Many of the spectators who had been queuing to get into the Tower since the early hours had never accepted Anne Boleyn as their queen anyway and still held to the claims of the late Katherine of Aragon and her daughter Mary.

Now they were hoping to see the upstart Boleyn woman's downfall.

In charge of it all was the Duke of Norfolk.

'He's the Lord High Steward now,' Kit's father whispered to him. 'Only appointed on Friday, mind.'

Kit had never seen this man before; he had a long thin face and hooded eyes and was dressed in ermine in spite of the warm May day. He wore a great gold chain of office and sat under a decorated cloth, with his son, the Earl of Surrey, at his feet.

'He looks very severe,' said Kit.

'He is trying to show he is not biased,' said the Ravenmaster. 'He is the queen's uncle.'

The queen's uncle! thought Kit. *Two aunts to spy on her and an uncle to be her judge. What a family!*

'The one who told her about the king's fall, when she lost the baby?'

'That's the one,' said his father.

There was a flurry of noise in the hall and Sir William Kingston, the constable, brought in the prisoner. Accompanied by Lady Kingston and her aunt, Lady Boleyn, Queen Anne looked composed as she walked to the chair provided for her.

The Sergeant-at-Arms called in the peers who were to pass judgement on their queen and her brother. There were many of them and even Thomas Wagstaffe didn't know them all but Kit recognised the Duke of Suffolk: he was the man who had rushed to take off the king's armour when he fell at Greenwich in January. Everything seemed to link back to that day.

There was one other lord who interested Kit. 'That's Henry Percy, the Earl of Northumberland,' his father told him, pointing out a rather sickly looking man, of about the poet's age.

The queen's betrothed, thought Kit. *Is is right for him to judge her?*

The indictment was read out: it went on and on, accusing the queen of things that made Kit blush. Anne Boleyn, however, sat silent and still, pale as the white lace at her neckline.

The names of the men, four of them already condemned to death, were given with very precise details of dates and places when and where they were supposed to have done terrible things with the queen. She had given them gifts of clothes and money and jewels, the charges said, and the men had grown jealous of one another. 'Sweet words, touches and otherwise' the queen was said to have bestowed on her courtiers.

But the only time she raised her eyes was when the charge was read out that 'the queen and these other traitors at Westminster, conspired the death and destruction of the king, the queen often saying she would marry one of them as soon as the king died, and affirming that she would never love the king in her heart'.

Kit thought he saw Anne's mouth silently frame the word 'No'.

The queen answered in a clear voice 'Not guilty' to all the charges in the long list. And when she was questioned more closely, she denied ever being unfaithful to the king or promising to marry Henry Norris or anyone else.

'Yes, I gave them presents,' she admitted. 'But that is the way of the court, as every one of my lords here assembled know. They were my husband's friends and I wanted to honour them.'

The peers shifted uncomfortably on their benches. The queen was impressing them, Kit could tell – but would it be enough? Could they defy the king?

She was asked if she had poisoned Katherine of Aragon or plotted to poison the Lady Mary, though Kit hadn't heard that in the list of charges. He wondered if it would make her angry but the queen just answered 'No' as she had to all the questions apart from the one about presents.

Kit remembered back to when he had heard about the old queen's death in January. It was only four months ago! And now the new queen was fighting for her life.

It was treason to imagine the king's death, if it went as far as wishing it or planning it – and the queen had admitted saying something to Henry Norris about it at the end of April – about how he would like to step into dead men's shoes 'if aught but good should befall the king'.

So that's why the king wouldn't go to Calais, thought Kit, *and why he took Norris out of the tournament!*

'It was a jest,' said the queen.

But no one in the hall was laughing.

The king believed his queen had caused all sorts of ills to attack his body, the prosecutor said. But Anne looked at him with barely concealed contempt.

'A man might have ills befall him without blaming his wife, I should hope,' she said. 'Even a king.'

Kit couldn't help admiring her spirit but he doubted that it was a wise thing to say.

At last the questioning stopped and the queen and

her women were allowed to withdraw. The jury of peers went into a room off the hall.

But they were away only as long as it took to take some refreshment and relieve themselves. It seemed to Kit no time at all till the nobles were filing back and the prisoner recalled.

Each lord was asked his verdict from the youngest to the most senior.

'Guilty,' said the first.

There was a sharp intake of breath all round the hall. But as every single peer said the same, there was no more noise until they reached the Duke of Suffolk, the last and oldest of the Peers of the Realm.

'Guilty.' He added his vote to the other twenty-five.

Kit heard how vindictively he said the damning word.

'Suffolk has always been against the Boleyns,' whispered Kit's father.

The Duke of Norfolk pronounced the sentence. To be taken to prison in the Tower and then, at the king's command, to the green within the Tower and there to be burned or beheaded as shall please the king.

He wept as he said it but all Kit could think was that the duke was a terrible hypocrite to cry as he condemned his niece to death.

And there were angry murmurings among the crowd.

'Burning or beheading?' said some of the peers. 'You can't have a sentence like that.'

'It's usually burning for treason for a woman,' said Thomas Wagstaffe.

'But we already know about the French swordsman,' said Kit.

He couldn't believe that he could still stand and speak. The worst he had feared had happened.

The great axe was turned so that the blade faced towards the queen.

But Anne was still calm and firm. She stood to make her statement.

'I am ready to die,' she said. 'But I am sorry for the loyal and innocent men who must die with me and because of me. I know I have not always been as humble and respectful towards the king as I should have been and I have sometime been a jealous wife but as God is my witness I have done him no other wrong.'

There was silence in the hall.

'All I ask is some time to make my peace with God,' added the queen.

And then she was gone.

Kit realised he had been holding his breath for a long time.

There was a commotion among the peers and he saw that Harry Percy had fainted. In all the disturbance, Kit slipped out of the hall. He needed some fresh air and he didn't feel at all sorry for the Earl of Northumberland. Percy had just declared his first love guilty of treason and condemned her to a horrible death one way or another.

Only now was it sinking in; Kit could hardly feel his

legs and had to sit down suddenly on the grass. When would it happen? He had to do whatever he could to save the princess so that he could reassure the queen before she faced her own death.

There was still the trial of the queen's brother to come and Kit felt he must go back inside, even though there wasn't much doubt about the verdict.

George Boleyn, Viscount Rochford, was as calm as his sister and dressed in full finery. Kit could see he was determined to put on a good show.

'Not guilty,' he said loudly and clearly to every charge.

As the trial wore on, with Rochford denying all the accusations levelled against him, there was a strange feeling in the crowd: Boleyn was doing well; Boleyn might be acquitted.

But when the peers were asked for their verdicts, again each one pronounced him guilty. All except Harry Percy, who had not come back into the hall.

Again, the Duke of Norfolk pronounced the sentence on his own kin: to be imprisoned in the Tower then taken to Tyburn for the hanging, drawing and quartering that was the standard punishment for treason.

George Boleyn seemed scarcely to have heard.

'All men must die, my lords,' he said. 'It is not given to many to know the hour of his death. I pray that His Grace the King will pay my debts for me so that no one will be left ruined by my departure from the world.'

Kit thought he was rambling – the viscount took a

list out of his doublet and read out the names of people he owed money to.

'It takes people different ways,' said his father. 'You'd better go now, Kit. I must help escort the peers away.'

Kit was glad to leave. He went straight to see the ravens. All six were waiting for him and made soft clicking noises with their beaks when they saw he had been crying.

'It is bad news?' asked Bran.

'The worst,' said Kit, flinging himself down on the grass beside the birds. He had thought he didn't care about the queen's brother – a man he had never seen before today – but now all he could think of was that five men as well as the queen were going to their deaths so that the king could marry a third wife.

How had it all happened so quickly?

'Do you remember the day the king brought you here, Blodwen?' he asked her.

'I do,' she said. 'I was very frightened. And then your father put me in a cage next to Bran. I have not been frightened since.'

'You remember how happy the king and queen were together?' said Kit. 'All dressed in yellow and free from care?'

'We all saw them,' said Bran.

'Then how can it be that four months later the king hates her and she is going to be killed within days?'

The birds gathered round him in a circle.

'It is not the way that ravens behave,' said Huginn. 'We can't pretend to understand.'

Kit dragged himself to his feet.

'I must go and see the poet,' he said. 'Though I think he and I can understand it no better than ravens do. I will see you in the morning.'

It was the first time since he met him that Kit found the poet sitting down. He was bowed over in his chair, holding his head in his hands. Kit could see straight away that he had heard the judgements.

When he heard Kit enter the room, Thomas Wyatt raised his head, showing bloodshot eyes and uncombed hair.

'You were there?' he asked. 'You were able to get in?'

Kit nodded. 'My father got me in at the back where he was standing guard.'

'Tell me.'

So Kit told him everything he could remember of the trial, ending with the great axe being turned towards George Boleyn as it had towards his sister the queen.

'But, since we hope the king will show mercy to the other men over their sentences,' he said, 'I am hoping he too will suffer no worse than beheading.'

'And Anne?' asked the poet. 'Surely the king won't let her burn like a common heretic?'

Kit reminded him about the swordsman from Calais.

'Calais was where all her troubles began,' said

Wyatt. 'If only her family had been content for her to stay at home and not become a court lady . . .'

Kit could tell he was wondering what would have happened if Anne had never caught King Henry's eye and had been allowed to marry her poet, though that could have happened only if his first wife had died.

Thomas Wyatt seemed to make a decision and pull himself together.

'Come, Kit,' he said. 'You can see now that there is only one thing left for us to do. I shall write you a letter. We can do nothing more for the queen except pray for her. But we can do something for her daughter.'

He went over to his table and swept aside the papers he had been working on, taking a fresh sheet.

'I know you are afraid to do it, but now you really must go and tell the secretary what you know.'

15

The Cleverest Man in England

When Isabel saw Kit early next morning, she knew he had not slept.

'You take it so hard, Kit,' she said. 'But what could you or anyone else do to stop it?'

'Have you made the special loaves?' he asked, his voice sounding rusty and unfamiliar to his own ear.

'They are all ready for you in this basket,' she said. 'The queen will be pleased to see you.'

'I am dreading it,' he said. 'But I have to do other things today that I am not looking forward to either.'

The queen was at a table busily writing when Kit came in with the bread.

'You are late, boy,' said Lady Kingston, taking the basket from him.

The next time I see you, you will be sprawled like a drunk on the floor, thought Kit.

He caught the queen's eye and bowed deeply to her. She gave him a small smile and he had the feeling she had read his thought.

His parents knew what Kit was going to do next.

'Do you want me to come with you?' his father had asked that morning.

'No. Will is going to take me to see his master and I have the poet's letter. I can manage. It might look suspicious if you left the Tower too. Someone might follow us. No one takes any notice of a boy like me.'

But as he walked out of the main gate to meet Will, Kit had the feeling he was being followed. It persisted all the way to the secretary's house. Eventually he looked up and saw two black shapes in the air above his head. Too high to tell which they were but it comforted him to know the ravens were looking out for him.

'It will be all right,' said Will, as they walked through the streets, though he sounded anxious himself. 'My master is no monster, even though I know some people see him that way. He arranged for me to be taught to read and write. He wants all the boys in his household to have a better life.'

'I am sure now that the king knows nothing of the plot,' said Kit. 'But can we be certain that the secretary is not behind it? He sends messages to that lord even if he does pull a face about him.'

'It is our only chance to do anything,' said Will. 'We can't get near the king.'

Kit felt the gold coin now safe in his jerkin. He had

been as close to the king on two occasions as he was to Will now. Perhaps he should have told Henry about the plot against Princess Elizabeth when he met him outside the Tower? The very thought was so terrifying that it made his coming meeting with Thomas Cromwell seem just a bit less frightening.

The boys had to wait. Kit could imagine what a flurry of activity there must be at the secretary's desk the morning after a queen had been condemned to death. One of the other boys told Will that Cromwell was cross not to find him when he wanted to send a message earlier.

'Then he will be in a bad mood with you,' whispered Kit.

'No,' said Will. 'Not when he hears what you have to tell him.'

At last, after such a long wait that Kit worried he wouldn't get back to the Tower in time to talk to the queen while her women slept, Will tugged at his jacket and took him up to his master's office. Will tapped on the door and dragged Kit in with him before his friend had time to think.

'There you are at last!' said the secretary. He looked tired and did not seem to be in a good mood. 'Who is this?'

'It is my friend Kit Wagstaffe from the Tower,' said Will. 'He is the Ravenmaster's boy.'

Cromwell looked him up and down appraisingly. Even on a day like this one, he was always watching and learning.

'And what can I do for the Ravenmaster's boy?' he said at last.

'I am a friend to the queen,' said Kit.

'That is a dangerous thing to be today,' said Cromwell. 'She does not have many friends – or many who would admit to it now.'

'And Thomas Wyatt is also my friend,' said Kit.

'You have surprising friends for a boy of your age and station,' said Cromwell.

'I have something important to tell you,' said Kit. 'It's about danger to the Princess Elizabeth.'

He had said it now. The secretary got up and went to the door, checking that there was no one listening outside.

'And why should I believe anything the Ravenmaster's boy tells me?' he said, sitting heavily back down at his desk. He had small, piggy eyes, but Kit could see why people called him the cleverest man in England; he was as alert and intelligent as if he hadn't been awake all night.

That's something we have in common, thought Kit. *He has had no more sleep than I have.*

But Will was answering his master. 'I can vouch for Kit's honesty,' he said.

Then Kit remembered the poet's letter. 'And I have this from Thomas Wyatt,' he said, holding it out to the secretary.

Cromwell read it in silence.

'I take Will's recommendation just as seriously as Wyatt's,' he said eventually. 'But the poet tells me that you will give me all the details in person. And that it was you who discovered the plot. So, Kit, tell me how you came by your information.'

This was the moment Kit had been dreading. A lot of people now knew about his ability to communicate with the ravens but would someone like Secretary Cromwell believe him? It would sound fantastic to his own ears to hear himself say it.

'I am a friend to the queen,' he repeated, 'and she asked me to find out what I could about her daughter – whether she was well looked after and happy. This was earlier, before the trials.'

'And how did you do this?'

'I have a . . . system of spies, sir.'

In spite of the seriousness of their conversation, the secretary smiled.

'I can see you are a considerable person, Kit Wagstaffe,' he said. 'Perhaps you should come and work for me when your father can spare you?'

'I can't tell you how I got the information, sir, but I can tell you who is plotting to kidnap the princess – and worse.'

And he told Thomas Cromwell a name that made his eyebrows almost disappear into his hair.

'I know that you know him, sir,' Kit added. 'Will you help?'

And that was it. The moment when he would find out whether the king's secretary would save the queen's daughter or was party to the plot himself.

'How can you doubt it?' asked Cromwell. 'Tell me everything.'

By the time Kit got back to the Tower his heart was lighter than it had been for days. But he was very late going up to see the queen and Alice was anxiously waiting for him.

'I thought you had deserted me like everyone else,' said the queen.

'Where are your women?' asked Kit. There was no sign of any of them.

'We had a little difficulty there,' said the queen. Incredibly, she was almost giggling. 'I had a message to say that the Archbishop of Canterbury wanted to see me and you could imagine what my aunts and the others were like. What would Thomas Cranmer say to see the constable's wife and all the other respectable ladies with their skirts all in disarray and their mouths open as they snored?'

'What did you do?' asked Kit, horrified.

'Alice helped me put them in my sleeping chamber. They could still just about walk if guided.'

The queen smiled at the thought and Kit wondered how she could be so merry so close to her death.

'What did the archbishop say?' he asked, wondering if he had been sent to pardon the queen; that would account for her mood.

'Not much,' she said. 'He wanted me to agree that the king and I had never been married. That was all, wasn't it, Alice? So that he could pronounce our marriage annulled. Making me no longer queen and my daughter no longer a princess. Oh and the king free to re-marry, of course.'

'Oh, Your Grace,' said Alice. Kit saw she had been crying.

'Do not look so stricken, Kit,' said the queen. 'It is not so surprising.'

'What did you tell the archbishop?' he asked.

'What could I say? After all, he was the one who proclaimed our marriage valid three years ago.'

'But if you had agreed, then maybe the sentence of the court would not be carried out,' said Kit. He thought he saw a glimmer of a way out.

'I have little hope of that,' said the queen.

Kit remembered what Cromwell had told Will about the lion being denied his haunch of venison. Had he devised a new way to get the king and queen divorced? Had he found the other meat that would satisfy the king?

'I saw you at the back of the court,' the queen said. 'It was good of you to come.'

'I thought you were magnificent, my lady,' he said.

'My Raven Knight,' she said, laying her hand on his arm. 'I'm sorry you had to hear those terrible things said about me. They are all lies, you know.'

'I know,' said Kit.

'Have you any news of my daughter?' she asked. 'It is all that I care about now.'

'No more direct news, ma'am,' said Kit, 'but I am

hopeful that she is in good health. I have people looking out for her.'

'You are a very remarkable boy, Kit,' said the queen. 'Don't you think so, Alice? Will you be Alice's knight when I am gone?'

'Please don't talk about being gone, ma'am,' said Alice.

'No, you are right. It is morbid. I am still hopeful that the king will show mercy.'

Kit wondered if she was talking about the sword.

'I have written to Sir William Kingston,' she said. 'I have offered to go into a nunnery to make things easier for my husband. What more can I do?'

There was no one waiting to escort Alice home so Kit took her.

'Everything is in chaos in the Tower since yesterday,' she said. 'I don't think anyone knows exactly what will happen and when. It is all so dreadful.'

'You should never have had to live through such times,' he said. 'You are too young for it.'

Alice stopped. 'I am the same age as you, Kit Wagstaffe!' Then she relented. 'We are both too young for it. And Isabel too. She has been wonderful about the bread. You couldn't have spoken privately to the queen without her.'

Kit thought about the waiting women all piled on the bed in the queen's chamber. He started to laugh.

'It must have been a sight to see – all those women snoring on the queen's bed!'

Alice smiled too and soon they were both bent double and crying with laughter.

'It was so funny,' gasped Alice. 'Knowing the archbishop was coming up the stairs any minute. And it was like pushing great big bolsters around.'

'What on earth is the matter with you two?'

George loomed in their path, glaring.

'The lord lieutenant sent me to see what had happened to Alice, as she is late getting back home.'

They were instantly sober. There was nothing funny about George Atwood.

'I am escorting her, as you see,' said Kit.

'And telling her crude jokes, by the look of it,' said George. 'Have you no respect? It is a solemn time in the Tower.'

Kit had put up with enough from George; he didn't need him to say how serious things were.

'We have been with the queen,' he said. 'There is nothing more solemn than her fate, is there? And yet *she* can jest.'

'Well, I don't see what she has to jest about,' said George. 'She's done for, isn't she?'

'Come on, Alice,' said Kit, pushing past George. 'You need to get home.'

'And what were you doing talking to the queen anyway, a boy like you?' continued George. 'She asked for Alice, I know, but Alice is a gentlewoman. I wonder what the lieutenant would say if he knew a boy like you had been closeted with the queen.'

Kit ignored him; he had more serious things to worry about than George.

He just hoped that the secretary had done as he had promised and sent messengers and extra guards to Hunsdon. It was out of his hands now. All he could do was send some ravens back to Hunsdon to check.

As soon as he had left Alice at her lodgings and shaken off George, Kit went back to where he had last seen the ravens. There were three, pecking about in the grass.

'You seem more cheerful, Kit,' said Blodwen.

He felt enormously fond of all the ravens, who cared so much about him and tried to help in any way they could.

The other two ravens were Huginn and Muninn.

'Where is Bran?' Kit asked. 'And which of you followed me out of the Tower this morning?'

'That was Bess and Thomas,' said Huginn. 'Bran told them to look out for you. But they have been back some time.'

Just then, Bran himself flew down and settled next to Blodwen with a loud 'Qu'aark'.

'Was your visit to the secretary successful?' he asked.

'It was, Your Majesty,' said Kit. 'Cromwell is sending to Hunsdon today. I think the princess will be safe.'

'That is good,' said Bran. 'I have heard news that makes me fear there is nothing more to be done for the queen.'

'What?'

'A starling from Chelsea,' said Bran. 'It is a bird we have used often before, one of the most intelligent of their kind.'

'What did it say?'

'We have had birds listening at the window of Jane Seymour for the last couple of days,' said Bran. 'Not that they know that is what she is called. But it was a fine day yesterday and in the morning she had her window open when a letter came from the king.'

'The bird is sure it was from the king?'

'He said it had a big wax seal with lions and flowers on it.'

'That's sounds like the king's crest.'

'There was a man in the room with her when the letter was brought – perhaps one of her brothers? The starling said he had the same colour feathers and shape of beak. Anyway, she read out the letter to him.'

'What did it say?'

'The lady said, "He says that by three of the clock this afternoon, the queen will be found guilty." And the man smiled and said, "Then there will be a new queen very soon," and took the letter from her.'

'Yesterday morning you say?' asked Kit. 'But that was *before* the trial.'

'Exactly,' said Bran. 'You see there was never any chance of saving the queen. It had all been decided in advance.'

16

Tower Hill

Kit's father looked grim the next morning.

'It is the fatal day,' he said.

'For the queen?' asked Kit.

'For the men,' said his father.

'But Lord Rochford was condemned only the day before yesterday! Is he to die with the others, with no delay and no mercy?'

'So it seems,' said the Ravenmaster.

Then the queen will not be long behind her brother, thought Kit.

'Are you to be on duty?' he asked.

'I am. That is how I know what is to happen today. They will be executed at Tower Hill.'

'So not Tyburn?' asked Kit. 'Does that mean beheading? George Boleyn has escaped the full sentence too?'

'I believe so,' said Thomas Wagstaffe. 'He will be the first to die.'

'Will you tell me all about it afterwards?' asked Kit. 'I want to know.'

'It won't be a fit tale to tell a boy,' said his mother. 'Or to tell anyone, come to that. Five comely men, two of them only in their twenties – I can't bear to imagine it.'

'Then don't imagine it, Mother,' said Kit, taking her hands, though he knew he would be doing exactly that.

There was a loud knock at the door and another Yeoman Warder stood there, looking flustered.

'I am almost ready,' said the Ravenmaster.

'It is the boy I am sent for,' said the warder.

Kit's heart started to pound in his chest. He felt as if he were about to be dragged off to the block himself. He had done so many wrong things in the last week he couldn't imagine which of his dangerous exploits had caught up with him.

His parents stood protectively in front of him.

'It's the secretary at the gate,' said the warder.

'Come to see the executions?' asked Kit's father.

'No. Come to fetch the boy. Sent me to get him and is in haste. Still sitting on his horse at the gate, so Kit had better hurry.'

'He is going nowhere with that devil without Cromwell explaining himself to me,' said Marjorie.

Thomas Wagstaffe laughed.

'I don't fancy the chances of the secretary against my wife,' he said. 'Do you know what this is about, Kit?'

Kit shook his head. Knowing it was Cromwell at the gate did not make him feel any more comfortable.

This was the man that everyone believed had arranged the queen's downfall, including the queen herself.

In the end, the whole family went down to the Court Gate. There Cromwell sat easily on a huge bay horse but he dismounted when he saw Marjorie and took off his hat.

'Do I have the honour of addressing Mistress Wagstaffe?' he asked.

Kit's mother dropped the merest curtsey.

'And the Ravenmaster too,' said Cromwell. 'You have a fine son, both of you.'

Kit felt his ears turning red.

But Cromwell was continuing. 'We probably should not talk about it here in the open but Kit has been very helpful and I would like to take him to Hunsdon with me.'

Hunsdon! thought Kit. *He is going to deal with it himself.*

'I promise to return him safely at the end of the day,' the secretary added.

So not the block this time, thought Kit, running his forefinger round his collar.

'How will you take him?' asked Marjorie, still trying not to be impressed.

'On my horse, if he'll let me,' said Cromwell, smiling.

And before Kit had time to think, he had been slung up on to the horse's neck in front of Thomas Cromwell. He couldn't pretend it was comfortable and it was bound to be worse after a ride of more than twenty miles but it was a bit thrilling to look down at the upturned faces of his parents and know that the strong arms around him that held the reins were those of a man with such power.

There was a harsh cry above them and Kit called out in Raven to two birds circling the Court Tower.

'We are off to Hunsdon! Come with us!'

Cromwell looked at him with keen interest.

Kit didn't know which ravens they were but he hoped it was two of the magical ones; he thought he could do with all the help he could get.

'Farewell!' said Cromwell, as the horse trotted away from the Tower and they turned towards the road north.

'I hope he'll be all right,' said Marjorie.

'I'm just glad he will be away from this place today and all the blood that will be shed here,' said her husband.

'Why are we going to Hunsdon?' asked Kit. 'Were your messengers not successful?'

'I rather hope we might catch the lord's hired men in the act,' said Cromwell. 'And I should like to question them myself.'

Kit said nothing to that. The secretary's questionings were legendary; not many men who had come under his interrogation failed to incriminate themselves and others. But it was also said he did not use torture – he never needed to.

'But today?' said Kit. 'I thought it would not be until the day of the queen's death.' It was the first time he had fully admitted to himself that such a day was coming.

'You are not the only one with a network of spies, Kit,' said Cromwell. 'My information is that it will be today. The execution of five men and one of them the queen's brother is enough to keep all eyes on the Tower.'

Kit guessed he was right. He squirmed himself into a slightly more comfortable position.

'Have you ridden a horse before?' asked the secretary.

'No, sir, and I don't really think I am doing so now.'

'Well, try not to wriggle, lad. We don't want you ending up over his head.'

They stopped only once on the way, so that Kit could have a stretch and both of them clear the dust from their throats with a drink at an inn. Then on to Hunsdon.

Riding a horse was something Kit had never imagined doing, though he had often wondered what it would be like to fly. He thought it might be like this, as they passed so quickly through streets it would have taken hours to trudge along. First houses, then trees and fields flew past, making Kit feel powerful and in control of the journey, although in fact he was squashed and terrified for most of it.

It was not too long before Kit saw the impressive gateway, with its heraldic beasts and the high tower beyond, topped by its gilded weathervane.

Cromwell didn't halt his mount at the gate but walked the horse quietly round the walls to a back entrance. He didn't go in here either and instead turned into a wooded area at the back. Here he slid out of the saddle and helped Kit down. He tied the horse's reins loosely to a tree so that the beast could eat the grass, then surprised Kit by taking food from his saddlebags.

'Here, Kit,' he said. 'We shall have a feast of the hunt.'

'What are we hunting?' asked Kit, as the secretary unpacked bread and cheese, a meat pie and a few of last autumn's apples.

'Not animals but people,' said Cromwell. 'Though I prefer most animals to the people we are after.'

'Are you sure they will attack today?'

'I think it is highly likely. All attention will be on the Tower today and the fate of the queen is now assured.'

Kit had almost forgotten that he hated Thomas Cromwell.

He thought of the queen in her lodgings and hoped that she could neither see nor hear anything of what was happening to the five men whose lives were ending because of her. Kit believed her with all his heart when she said the accusations against her were lies.

Cromwell was looking at him as if he knew what Kit was thinking.

'It was the king's will,' he said.

'That his daughter would be attacked?'

'That his wife would be disposed of.'

'He wants another wife, doesn't he?'

'He does. And that's all you need to understand about the queen's situation.'

'Was there no one to stand up for her and tell him he was doing wrong?'

The king's secretary sighed.

'I like you, Kit. I like the way that things seem so simple and straightforward to you. But believe me, if you knew it was your head or hers, I think you would have done the same as I did.'

Kit opened his mouth to protest. But he thought of his young neck on the block and the axe coming down on it, maybe not aiming true the first time or two and mashing up bone and blood and sinew. And he was silent.

'May you never be in such a terrible place, where you have to make such a choice,' said Cromwell. 'Now, have some pie.'

Kit heard a croaking and looked up. There were two big black birds in the trees above them. Bran and Muginn. He cawed to them softly and they flew down and walked on the grass, eating the crumbs Kit threw for them.

'You have a special kind of friendship with animals,' said Cromwell.

'Well, I do like animals,' said Kit. 'But it's only the ravens that I can . . . ah, talk to and understand.'

'And I am beginning to understand about your network of spies,' said Cromwell. 'How useful to be able to send eyes and ears anywhere you like, through the air.'

'Qu'aark!' said Muginn warningly. 'Men coming.'

Kit and the secretary scrambled to their feet and Cromwell put a finger to his lips. They crept forward to the edge of the trees.

And there were the three men Kit had seen in

the London inn with the lord's steward. He wondered what the secretary would do if the men scaled the wall. Cromwell was a very solid, stocky man, but there was only one of him; Kit was not as good with his fists as George Atwood.

But Cromwell waited while two of the men went over the wall, helped by a grumbling third. So that was their plan: two to do the deed and a third to keep watch. Several long minutes elapsed while the third man cursed and muttered; it had certainly been an effort hoisting his conspirators up and over and he was panting heavily.

Before he had a moment to collect himself, Cromwell was on him, one large hand over his mouth, the other twisting an arm behind his back.

'Put your hand in my belt, boy,' he said to Kit. 'There's a knife there – hold it against his ribs for me.'

The man's eyes were mostly whites as he realised the jig was up.

'Now,' said Cromwell, 'I am going to take my hand away from your mouth and use it to hold the dagger my young friend has pressed against your heart. You will be as silent as a mouse. More silent – no squeaks.'

The man tried to nod but Cromwell's burly arm was round his neck.

'You don't need to say anything,' said the secretary. 'We know about Arthur Burford. All you need to do is stay quiet while I bind your arms. Fetch the rope, boy.'

Kit wondered if the man had any idea whose arms

were clamped on him like an iron cuff, as he ran back to the horse and took the rope from its pommel.

The intruder was soon bound and gagged with one of the secretary's handkerchiefs and rolled out of sight, hidden in the trees.

Cromwell then took a key and opened the back gate of Hunsdon Manor, laughing when he saw Kit's expression.

'I have my methods too, you see! Now come – there is no time to lose if we are to catch them in the act.'

It didn't take Kit long to realise that the secretary had not just sent messages and guards to Hunsdon but had alerted everyone to be ready for the attack on this day. They ran across the gardens at the back and were just in time to see one of the men levering open a window on the ground floor. After them came some of the extra men the secretary had sent to the manor house.

'We don't need to do that, Kit,' puffed Cromwell, swerving round to a back door where a servant was waiting. They pounded up the stairs to the first floor and along a gallery where Cromwell briefly lifted his hat to a young woman and her attendant. Kit wondered if it had been the Lady Mary – the daughter of the old queen.

They burst into a room where Lady Bryan was with great composure holding on to a child with red-gold curls, while two rough men tried to pull her out of the woman's arms.

'I arrest you in the name of the king!' thundered Cromwell. The guards rushed in and had soon tied the kidnappers up in their own rope. They had brought more than enough to truss up one small child – and a sack to put her in.

'There's another one tied up in the wood at the back gate,' Cromwell told the guards.

The little princess seemed to think it was all a good game and didn't stop her chattering and playing the whole time.

So this was Anne's daughter! Kit could see nothing of the queen in her; her colouring and features were so like the king's. He stared at her, drinking in every detail to tell the queen the next time he saw her. The next time . . . Kit realised it would probably also be the last. He sat down suddenly on a footstool and realised that he was shaking.

Cromwell was playing with the little girl, who clearly knew him and let him pick her up and swing her round. How could he? This was the man who was ensuring that the child's mother would very soon be dead. But one thing Kit realised: the secretary could never have been part of a plot to harm a child.

After they had taken refreshments and walked back to the horse, Kit asked what would happen to the men.

'They will be tried for treason, of course,' said Cromwell. 'For seeking to abduct and doubtless harm a royal princess.'

'But is she still a princess?' Kit asked.

Cromwell stopped. 'You are a clever boy, Kit,' he said. 'At this moment I do not know. Perhaps she isn't.

But she is a child under royal protection still, as far as I am concerned, and those scoundrels deserve everything that is coming to them.'

'What about the steward? And the lord?'

'Oh, I shall have some fun with them,' said Cromwell, looking like a plump cat who had some juicy mice in prospect. 'They will hear that the plot has been uncovered and the men arrested, but they won't know that I know of their involvement. It will be a useful tool to employ against them when I need one.'

That night, Kit told the poet that the princess was safe.

'I shall tell Her Majesty tomorrow morning,' he said.

'Well done!' said Wyatt, clapping him on the shoulder. 'It will be a great relief to her.'

But he looked very pale and could not eat his supper.

'Did your father attend the day's executions?' he asked.

Kit had known he would have to pass on the Ravenmaster's account of what he had seen but had put it off for as long as possible, filling in every detail of the princess's rescue first.

'It was as you might expect,' he told Thomas Wyatt. 'Lord Rochford first.'

'I heard it took three blows to take off George's head,' said the poet with a shudder.

Thomas Wagstaffe had not held back any of the details but Kit had hoped that Wyatt could have been spared that one.

'The other four men died cleanly,' he said.

'Aye – good fortune for young Smeaton. The others had given the headsman practice before him.'

It was as if the poet would have preferred the musician to be hacked to death rather than the nobleman.

'I don't think it can have been good fortune to see all those bodies and heads and all that blood while he waited to die,' said Kit.

Wyatt just grunted. 'And none of them but Smeaton confessed any wrongdoing with the queen?' he asked.

'So my father said. Brereton came closest to claiming innocence. The others just asked pardon for general sins.'

'They couldn't say too much,' said the poet. 'They would worry about what might happen to their families if they spoke anything but respectfully of the king.'

He gave himself a shake.

'So much for them. It could have been me on that block today, Kit, since there was no more of a case against them than against me. I shall pray for their souls tonight and give thanks that I was spared.'

'Thanks to Cromwell?'

'To God – well, maybe acting through Cromwell. He could have brought me down if he had wanted to.'

'And he did come in person to make sure the princess was saved,' said Kit. 'I don't understand him.'

The poet laughed.

'No one understands him. Least of all the queen. You will see her tomorrow?'

'Yes. I think it will be for the last time.'

'Will you say goodbye to her from me? Tell her I did not forget her at the end?'

'I will. I will never forget her myself.'

17

The Last Day

Kit went early to the bakery; the ravens all accompanied him. Isabel had not put powder in the bread this time but Kit was going to stay and talk to the queen anyway. It was too late to worry about what her waiting women might tell anyone now.

Isabel handed him the basket and lent forward to give Kit a kiss. No words passed between them.

He walked to the queen's lodgings with all six big black birds following in a line behind him.

Like a funeral procession, Kit thought.

But he was glad they were there.

The guard nodded him through and Kit went up the stairs slowly.

'Good morning, Your Majesty,' he said.

There was no sign of Alice.

Normally he said nothing, which was what was expected of a servant.

'Hold your tongue, boy!' said one of the women.

'No – let you be quiet, Aunt Shelton,' said Anne Boleyn, coming to take the basket with her own hands. 'Good morning, Kit. But you must not say "Majesty" now. I have been informed that Archbishop Cranmer yesterday proclaimed my marriage to the king invalid. So I am no longer queen.'

'Then, Mistress Boleyn, if I must so call you, I have news of your daughter.'

'This is outrageous,' said Lady Shelton. 'The impudence of the boy! Lady Kingston, can you do nothing about this Tower servant?'

Another woman, one Kit recognised as the constable's wife, came forward but Anne stopped her too.

'I may no longer give orders as a queen but I insist that as a guest in the Tower and a woman doomed to die today, that you let me hear what news this kind boy brings me of my daughter. If you have a drop of compassion in your blood, you will leave him alone and not stop him from telling me his story.'

'Today?' said Kit. He felt the blood draining from his face and thought he would fall.

'So I believe,' said Anne. 'I have made my confession to the Archbishop himself and heard Mass.'

She was completely composed.

'I wanted you to know the princess is safe,' said Kit. 'There *was* some danger but Secretary Cromwell has doubled her guard and no harm will come to her.'

'Cromwell?' said Anne. 'My enemy?'

'He is no enemy to the princess, my lady. I rode to Hunsdon with him myself.'

'This boy is making up fairy tales,' said another of the women. 'Why would the king's secretary take such a rapscallion anywhere?'

'Hush, madam,' said Anne. 'I want to hear his tale. And this is no ordinary boy. Look out through the window if you don't believe me. I saw the ravens come with you, Kit. They know it is my last day.'

The birds were lined up in the courtyard outside. Something about their demeanour caused the waiting women to stop interfering.

'I fear my little Elizabeth is no longer a princess,' said Anne. 'She will be called Lady Elizabeth, like her half-sister Lady Mary. Oh, how I wish I had been kinder to Mary and even to her mother! I know what it means now to be the queen with her title stripped away and her love discarded for a new bride.'

Kit was silent. *At least the old queen had been allowed to live*, he thought, but he could hardly say it now.

'Even if your daughter loses her title,' he said eventually, 'I know from what happened yesterday that the secretary will continue to protect her. I hope it gives you some comfort?'

'It does, my Raven Knight. I know there are things you are concealing from me with your stories of danger but as long as that last is true, I am content. In fact, I feel ready to leave the world and all its deceits.'

The waiting women were tucking into their breakfast bread now and had given up taking notice of him. The queen, as he still thought of her, ate nothing. From the look of her, she had eaten little or nothing for days. Her skin was stretched so thinly over her bones that it looked almost transparent. Kit couldn't help but look at her neck.

She was aware of it and spoke to him in a low voice. 'It is a very little neck, is it not, Kit? It will not take much effort to cut through it.'

Kit prayed fervently that she had not heard about what happened to her brother.

As if following his thoughts, she went on, 'I hear that the men all died confessing their sins,' she said.

The men: it was as if one of them had not been her brother.

'But that poor wretch Mark did not withdraw what he said he had done with me,' she went on. 'And that leaves a terrible stain on my name. I wish he had taken it all back. He will suffer the torments of Hell for his lies.'

She turned to Lady Kingston. 'Your husband took the Host with me and heard me swear to my innocence. He knows I shall go to meet my Maker today punished for crimes I did not commit.'

Kit had never seen someone so close to death but he recognised that the former queen was moving further away from him, into a place where he couldn't follow her.

'And where is your husband now, Lady Kingston?'

she went on. 'He said my death would take place at noon. Surely he should be here soon?'

At noon! thought Kit. *A few short hours.*

He had to deliver his other message.

'My lady,' he said. 'I have a few words for you from Thomas Wyatt.'

'This is intolerable,' said Lady Shelton. 'That a servant boy should deliver messages from another prisoner!'

But Anne ignored her and so did Kit.

'Ah, if only I could have married Thomas Wyatt, Kit,' she said. 'I would not now be awaiting the executioner. We might have been happy, with a brood of children. But then I would not have been queen. Was it all worth it for just three years? What does he say?'

'He says to tell you that he will not forget you,' said Kit.

'I wonder if he will write poems about me,' said Anne. 'And about what I will suffer today.'

And then the constable of the Tower came into the room. Sir William Kingston frowned at Kit, who hastily snatched up the bread basket and made to leave.

'I come with news that ought to be welcome but I fear will not,' the constable said to Anne.

Kit made himself very small so that he would not be noticed.

'A pardon from the king?' asked Anne, her hand flying to her throat.

'I am afraid not,' said Kingston. 'It is that the . . .

ah . . . execution is postponed till tomorrow. Nine of the clock in the morning.'

'But you said that yesterday!' protested Anne. 'And I stayed up all night.'

'I am truly sorry, madam,' said Kingston, 'but those are my orders.'

'I must live a little longer then,' said Anne. 'But it will be a weary time till I am released from my troubles.'

She dabbed at a few tears.

This is so cruel, thought Kit. *If I had a powder that would kill her kindly I would give it to her now.*

And then he thought, *Mossy Meg!*

As soon as Kingston had gone, Kit took his leave of the former queen.

'I hope to come back and see you this afternoon,' he said.

'That would be good of you, Kit. I will need distraction.'

He ran down the stairs, aware that he might have missed a chance to say a proper goodbye, but full of his new idea.

There was no time to go home and tell his parents; Kit ran out of the main gate and raced to Mossy Meg's house as fast as he could, in some danger of losing his way.

He was out of breath by the time he reached the nondescript house and knocked on the door.

Please be in, please be there, he wished, as his heartbeat gradually slowed and his lungs filled with air again.

Meg was slow to open the door. She looked tired, with dark circles under her eyes. Kit wondered if she had some sort of link with Anne Boleyn that made her share the queen's thoughts and feelings.

'Hello, Kit,' she said. 'It's too late for more tainted bread. I thought she would be dead by now.'

'It's been put off till tomorrow morning,' he said. 'That's why I've come.'

'Has she asked for something from me?'

'No – it's my idea. Have you got anything that she could take that would ease her out of life without pain?'

'I doubt anything would be quicker and easier than one blow from the French executioner's sword.'

'Well then, something to help her face that end calmly?'

'I do,' said Meg. 'And it is better for you to take her this. Anything else would be too dangerous.'

She turned away to her shelves of jars and started to crush leaves in a mortar. Kit found the very smell calming and hoped it would help the woman he couldn't help thinking of as the queen.

'Tell her or her women to make an infusion with this,' said Meg. 'It will help her to sleep tonight. And another infusion in the morning to calm her on her way to death. There is enough here.'

She gave him a small bag, which he stuffed in his jerkin.

'And give her a message from me too. Tell her I shall

think of her and pray for her and light all the candles in my cottage at her last hour.'

Kit thanked her and left. He had never given Meg any money for her potions and he thought too late of the gold coin the king had given him, which was now back under his mattress.

When he got back to the Tower he saw warders turning people away and ushering other people out.

'What's going on?' he asked the guard on the gate.

'Orders from the secretary,' he said. 'No strangers allowed in the Tower – every foreigner must be out by morning. Good thing you are safely back from wherever you've been. The gates will all be locked tonight.'

Kit ducked in through the postern gate and decided he would call at the bakery on his way up to the queen's lodgings. This was Isabel's quiet time of day, when the ovens were allowed to cool for a few hours and preparations were made for early morning.

'Oh, Kit,' she said when she saw him. 'They say it will be tomorrow morning.'

Kit nodded. 'Come with me?' he asked her. 'I have brought her a soothing draught from Mossy Meg.'

Isabel wiped her hands on her apron and took it off. She smoothed her hair and straightened her skirt.

The two of them walked slowly up the stairs, knowing it was the last time they were likely to see Anne Boleyn alive. The guards had been so affected by the order to remove all strangers that they seemed quite willing to let anyone they knew pass into the queen's rooms.

Alice was there this time, waiting on Anne, and Kit was able to give her the herbal mixture without the other women seeing.

'This is my friend Isabel, my lady,' said Kit. 'She is the one who bakes your morning bread.'

Isabel dipped a curtsey.

'Then thank you, Isabel,' said Anne. 'I have nothing to give you but my thanks. I have already distributed the money that my husb— that the king sent me.'

'I don't expect even thanks,' said Isabel. 'It has been my pleasure to serve you.'

'You have nice friends, Kit,' said Anne. 'First Alice and then Isabel. You are lucky. There was a time when I had many friends – at least I thought so. Where are they now?'

Kit wanted to tell her about Meg but he didn't dare with the women listening; he didn't want to get Meg into any trouble.

In the end, there was no big farewell scene. Anne thanked them all again for their help.

'Especially my Raven Knight,' she said. 'I know what you have done and I am eternally grateful. I will soon know what eternity means too.'

She gave him a kiss on the cheek and embraced both the girls.

'Leave me now, all of you,' she said. 'I need to prepare myself.'

Alice gave her the herbs and whispered that she must take one draught that night and one in the morning.

The waiting women took no notice because Alice was the lieutenant's daughter. Kit hoped that meant she would be allowed the infusions.

The three friends left together. As the light faded in the Tower, they were united by a sense of loss and fear.

Kit took Alice back to her lodgings, which were next to the Bell Tower, where Thomas Wyatt was imprisoned, so he went up to see the poet afterwards, even though someone else had taken him his supper already.

Not that he had eaten anything. Kit found him brooding over a cup of wine.

'I gave her your message,' he said.

'Thank you. I'm glad she knows I will be thinking of her.'

'I should think everyone in London will be thinking of her – but perhaps not all very kindly.'

'The lieutenant has said I can watch from his rooms next door.'

'Do you want to?' asked Kit.

'I think I should try,' said Wyatt. 'And I think I could bear it – especially if you watch with me.'

18

Here to Die

Thomas Cromwell did not go to bed that night. Will Rede slept like a baby on the rug in front of the hearth in the secretary's office, as if he hadn't a care in the world. Cromwell put a coverlet over him in the cold early hours.

'Sleep on, boy,' he said. 'I wish I could.'

Across town, Meg was awake too, not drinking her own concoction; she wanted to keep vigil for the queen that was.

In the Tower, the poet paced up and down all night. Neither the constable nor the lord lieutenant got much rest either.

It was a momentous thing they would do on the morrow: kill a queen! Even if she had been stripped of her title, she had been anointed as queen three years earlier and such an execution had never happened before. It was to take place inside the Tower walls, not out on Tower Hill where the five men had died. That at least was Anne's due as former queen.

Alice was as wakeful as her father. She could hear him moving around restlessly and could imagine what he was thinking. The younger children slept on unaware.

Isabel was used to short nights, since she had to get up so early to stoke the ovens, and usually slept soundly for the few hours' rest she had. But not this night. She watched the sun rise on that morning, after her vigil, as so many others in the Tower did.

One of them was Kit. The day he had dreaded for weeks was ahead of him and he didn't want to go to sleep and wake up realising it was here.

In his lodging by the Lion Tower, George snored peacefully. But the bear in its cage shifted awkwardly, unable to settle. It thought it could smell blood on the air and had troubled dreams.

In the queen's lodgings, whether because of a herbal potion Anne had made for herself or just because of her vigil the night before, the former queen slept soundly, unaware of how many people were awake on her behalf.

It wasn't a high scaffold, less than four feet tall, but about a thousand people stood round the black-draped platform. All English people, in accordance with Cromwell's orders. He stood there, waiting, alongside the king's bastard son, Henry Fitzroy. The king now had three illegitimate children, Cromwell realised. He hoped the new queen would soon fulfil expectations and bear a legitimate male heir to the throne.

The Duke of Suffolk was in the front row, with Cromwell and Henry Fitzroy. He had loathed the Boleyns for as long as he could remember and his face was set and grim. After today there was no way they would ever be back in favour at court.

There was one person missing: the king would not come to witness Anne's death himself.

The lord lieutenant had escorted Thomas Wyatt to a room in his own lodgings, from which the scaffold could be seen. He looked a bit surprised to see Kit come to join the poet but Wyatt assured him he needed the boy and, since there were two guards outside the door, armed with halberds, Sir Edmund Walsingham left them and hurried down the stairs to do his unpleasant duty.

'Look at the crowd,' said Wyatt. 'They are here to see a woman's death as if it were a spectacle.'

'My father tells me this is what people do,' said Kit. 'Crowds came to see the old men beheaded last summer and plenty were on Tower Hill to watch the executions of the young men.'

'I know,' said Wyatt. 'But it is different when it is someone you know and believe to be innocent of all charges. Someone you once loved.'

'Can you see the ravens?' asked Kit, standing on tiptoe at the window.

'I can,' said the poet. 'But here, get up on this stool. Now you are the same height as me.'

'I can see them,' said Kit. 'All six. I have asked them to give me their accounts in case there are things I can't see – or can't bear to look at.'

Thomas Wyatt gripped his shoulder.

'Not long now,' he said.

It was no great distance from the queen's lodgings to the scaffold. Anne was a slight figure, dressed in grey with an ermine cloak over her dress and a scarlet kirtle underneath, walking past the King's Hall where so recently she had been on trial. It seemed much longer than three years ago that she had dined there the night before her coronation; a lifetime ago.

Sir William Kingston walked beside her, with a bodyguard of two hundred men.

'Do they think she'll try to escape now?' asked Kit, looking down on the procession.

'No – it is an escort fitting for her position,' said Wyatt.

There were some of her waiting women around her too but Kit couldn't tell which ones with all the soldiers surrounding them.

When they reached the scaffold, the constable helped Anne up the few steps.

Kit gasped when he saw the swordsman step forward: it was really going to happen.

The woman he still thought of as queen stood at the edge of the scaffold and spoke to the crowd. Kit and Wyatt could not catch her words at the distance they were but they saw several people weeping, including her attendants.

They helped her remove her fur cloak and Anne took off her own headdress and let fall her hair – still black and glossy – which Kit remembered from her coronation. A woman handed her a white cap and she bundled her abundant locks up into it, giving the executioner a clear view of her white neck.

Kit saw Anne kneel in the straw that had been spread to catch her blood. Another woman blindfolded her eyes.

Thomas Wyatt's grip on Kit's shoulder became so tight that the boy later found himself covered in bruises.

Kit hadn't meant to watch the last moment but it came so quickly, catching him off guard.

One merciful swing of the great sword and Anne Boleyn fell headless to the ground.

Kit didn't know he had fainted until he found himself lying on the floor, having fallen off the stool he had been standing on. Thomas Wyatt was leaning over him, patting his face and looking worried. So they both missed what happened after the sword blow fell.

By the time Kit had struggled to his feet, protesting that he was quite all right, the spectacle by the White Tower was over and the crowd dispersing.

There were tears running down the poet's face.

'What an end!' he said. 'She was a lady most elegant and gracious.'

He stumbled away from the window and almost knocked into a table where the lieutenant had left a tray with a jug of wine and one goblet. With a shaking hand, he poured himself a draught and then offered some to Kit.

'You've had a shock,' he said. 'Take some wine.'

Kit did not normally drink wine but he took a big gulp, as if it had been small ale. He could feel it course down his throat into his stomach, warming him as it went. And he felt colour return to his cheeks. He didn't much like the taste but he could feel it was helping him recover.

But he also knew he would never forget what he had just seen.

George Atwood had muscled his way into the edge of the crowd and was now reporting everything to Isabel, as he sank his teeth into a juicy meat pie at the bakery.

Isabel tried not to listen but the bloody details flowed on.

'The women wrapped the head in a white cloth,' he was saying. 'But it was soon as red as her kirtle.'

Isabel could see it in her mind only too well. She wondered if Kit had seen it in reality.

'But what a shambles afterwards!' said George. 'Kingston is really not up to the job, you know. No coffin ready for her body. They had to empty the bow-staves out of a chest so that the women had something to put her remains in – body and head.'

'That doesn't sound very respectful,' said Isabel. 'Not for a queen.'

'Ah, but she wasn't a queen any more, was she? Not since yesterday. She was just a traitor.'

'Have you no compassion?' said a voice behind him.

Alice Walsingham had come back to the Palace buildings, drawn to the place where she had been waiting on the queen for the last few weeks.

George spat crumbs and turned red in the face. Alice was the person whose good opinion he most craved. And she was looking very angrily at him.

'I'm sorry, Mistress Alice,' he spluttered. 'You must have been close to her.'

'Even if I were not, you should not speak so of a soul just departed this life,' said Alice.

'Even a wicked one?' asked George unwisely.

'I don't know about that,' said Alice. 'It is not for us to judge. But I know that the queen wasn't wicked. Anyone who knew her knows that. You are just showing your ignorance – as well as a cruel nature.'

The Ravenmaster came to join them. He was as pale as Alice, but he had actually attended the execution, unlike Alice, who had been ordered by her father to stay in her room.

'Have you seen Kit?' he asked them. 'I am worried about him.'

'He is in my father's lodging, with the poet,' said Alice. 'I haven't seen him but I heard they were going to watch from a window what has passed this morning.'

'That was very wrong of Wyatt,' said Thomas Wagstaffe. 'It was no sight for a boy.'

'I think Kit wanted to be there,' said Alice.

'Did you see it?' asked Isabel.

'I did,' said the Ravenmaster. 'And I wish with all my heart that I had not. I wish Kit had told me what he was going to do. I shall go and find him.'

The ravens went with him.

The guards outside the room where Kit and the poet had watched Anne Boleyn's last minutes let Thomas Wagstaffe through; everyone in the Tower knew the Ravenmaster.

And they let him back out with his boy too.

'The lieutenant might not be back for hours,' he said. 'He has to entertain all the nobles who came. But I'd like to get my boy away from here. It will be enough for you to watch over Thomas Wyatt, won't it?'

He bundled Kit down the stairs and out into the fresh air. The boy was shaking even though it was not a cold day. Six ravens waited for them at the foot of the stairs and prukked round Kit as if he had been a precious chick.

Father and son walked across the Inner Ward, the Ravenmaster's arm round his boy's shoulders, but there was no way back to their lodgings that didn't pass between the scaffold and the chapel.

There were newly dug graves outside the chapel, where four of the five executed men lay headless. And a group of women was coming out of the main door; there was blood on their clothes and hands and they were all weeping.

Thomas Wagstaffe cursed under his breath. This was the last thing he wanted Kit to see.

'It's all right,' said Kit. 'I'm glad they are crying now. They were not kind to her when she lived.'

'Are you really all right, Kit?' asked his father. 'I wish I could have spared you what I saw and heard.'

'I heard nothing,' said Kit. 'Not from where we were. What did she say?'

'That she was not here to preach a sermon but had come here to die,' said the Ravenmaster. 'And to ask us to pray for her.'

'We can do that,' said Kit.

'And she praised the king for his gentleness and mercy.'

'Ha!' Kit snorted. 'I suppose she had to do that to protect her daughter.'

'Be careful what you say inside the Tower,' said his father. 'We must all protect ourselves. If it is ever known how close you were to the queen, you could be in danger yourself.'

'Thomas Cromwell knows,' said Kit, 'and no one is more dangerous than him – unless the king is here to listen to me?'

He was in a reckless mood; he had done everything he could and the queen was still dead.

As they passed, a group of people was coming out of the Cold Harbour Gate, through which Anne had walked to her death so shortly before. One of them was Thomas Cromwell.

'Speak of the devil,' said the Ravenmaster.

They stopped, hoping to be ignored by the secretary but he made straight towards them. Kit saw out of the corner of his eye that George Atwood was hovering nearby.

'Ravenmaster,' said Cromwell in greeting, 'and Master Kit.'

Kit looked down at his shoes. Although he was grateful to the secretary for acting so swiftly about the princess, he did not want to talk to him, or even acknowledge him on this morning. They couldn't even say 'This is a bad business' to each other, knowing that Cromwell had been behind it all.

'There is good news from Hunsdon,' said the secretary. 'The Lady Elizabeth is well and unharmed.'

'And an orphan,' said Kit, raising his face at last.

'Not so. She has a father and I promise I will not let him forget her.'

Kit bit his lip.

'You have a fine son, Wagstaffe,' said Thomas Cromwell quietly. 'Loyalty is a good quality. I would like to do something to help him – to take care of his education.'

Kit tried to mouth 'No' to his father but the Ravenmaster was not looking at him.

'That is most kind, sir,' he was saying. 'Kit, say thank you to the secretary.'

'Thank you,' said Kit. 'But there is no need. Thomas Wyatt has promised me the same.'

'Has he now?' said Cromwell. 'Well, Thomas Wyatt is a friend of mine and I think the two of us together may ensure a future worthy of your exceptional talents.'

He had spoken loudly enough for George to have heard him. Kit was ashamed that he felt pleased about that. That George had heard Cromwell's offer.

In fact, Kit realised, all his feelings were a mess. Here were people walking about and getting on with their lives when all he could think about was a sword swishing through the air and a woman falling, falling. In his mind he thought he would see her falling for ever.

'The boy doesn't look well,' he heard Cromwell's voice saying as if from very far away. 'You should take him home.'

Thomas Wagstaffe was much too polite to say that he had been doing that when the secretary stopped them, but he bowed and took his leave, half dragging Kit along after him.

'Exceptional talents, my arse,' Kit heard George say behind him. 'He can scarcely put one foot in front of the other. Just because the whore is dead! I saw her head fly off and you don't see me drooping about like that.'

Kit tried to say something but found that he couldn't frame the words. And after that, a blessed darkness descended and he could neither speak nor think any more.

19

The Way it Might Have Been

It was very quiet in the Tower for the rest of that day. Kit's parents put him to bed after his father had carried him across the Inner Ward. But even when he had woken up and eaten some broth, Kit could tell that there was a hush outside. After the dignitaries who had come to witness the execution of a queen had left, there were few people walking about.

The few visitors who had come to look at the scaffold and search for spots of blood on the cobbles stayed well away from where the Yeoman Warders had their lodgings.

Kit felt like someone getting over an illness but by the afternoon he could stay indoors no longer. He pulled on his clothes and went to find the ravens.

They clustered round him on the grass, clacking their beaks in sympathy.

'I am going to the chapel,' he said to them. 'Do you want to come with me?'

The big black birds lifted off into the air and flew the few hundred yards to where Saint Peter-in-Chains stood, the fresh graves outside it unadorned by any flowers.

I suppose I'll have to start trimming the ravens' flight feathers again now, thought Kit. *There is no more spying for them to do.*

There were a few visitors inside and outside the chapel but Kit was relieved to find Isabel and Alice both standing silently in the chancel looking down at a slab in the floor that had obviously only just been hastily put back in place.

'They are together now – brother and sister,' said Alice.

Kit was glad that the queen and her brother had been granted that much respect and were not sharing a few feet of earth with the courtiers outside. But he felt numb.

For the last two weeks – had it really been as little as that? – his whole life had been entangled with that of the queen and her daughter. Now he had no idea what to do next. His mind was as empty as if it had suffered the same fate as the queen's head.

He would care for the ravens, live quietly with his parents, continue to visit the poet until Wyatt was released from the Tower. And then what? The vision of himself as an educated man, perhaps learning to be someone important and well-to-do just kept falling out of his thoughts.

'What will you do now?' asked Isabel, as if she could read his mind.

'I don't know,' said Kit. 'I feel as if everything has come to an end.'

'Well it has for her,' whispered Isabel. 'But you can wager that everything will go on as before for the king. There will be a new queen and she had better be very careful if she doesn't want to end up in the same place!'

Outside the chapel, the ravens waited on the grass. Some visitors were pointing them out and talking about them.

Kit got nearer and heard them saying, 'Look at those birds! They hang round the scaffold hoping for blood to drink.'

'Qu'aark!' they all squawked and took off into the air.

'What are you talking about?' Kit said. 'I look after the ravens and they don't drink human blood. That's just nonsense.'

But something about the way the group were looking at him told him that not only would they not believe him, they were probably going to spread this gossip further. He could hardly tell them that he had asked the ravens to witness the execution and tell him about anything he had missed.

So he turned his back on them and walked back home. Isabel and Alice watched him go.

'That's the first time he hasn't offered to walk me home,' said Alice. 'He must be really upset.'

'Don't worry,' said Isabel. 'I'll walk with you.'

'It's only a few hundred yards,' said Alice. 'I never understood why my father wouldn't let me walk alone. It's quite safe inside the Tower.'

'Unless you are a queen,' said Isabel. 'But you're right about Kit – I've never seen him like this before.'

Thomas and Marjorie were worried too. Kit ate little of his supper and did not go to visit the poet. The Ravenmaster took Wyatt his food and wine instead.

'How is Kit?' was the poet's first question.

'Not better for watching the queen die,' said Wagstaffe. 'I could wish you had spared him that, sir.'

Wyatt was immediately contrite.

'I am so sorry,' he said. 'It was selfish of me. I thought we could help each other. He has done such a lot that I forgot he is still a boy.'

'Well, it's done now,' said Wagstaffe, unpacking the poet's supper. 'We've sent him to bed. I hope he doesn't have nightmares.'

Kit was in bed but not asleep. He was sure that if he closed his eyes for longer than a blink, he would see again the sight he most wanted to forget.

There was a tapping at his window and he looked up to see a gathering of black feathers. He went over to open the casement and in flew Bran, Huginn and Muninn – the three most extraordinary of the extraordinary ravens.

'We have come to keep you company,' said Bran,

perching at the foot of Kit's bed. 'We thought your dreams might be troubled tonight.'

Kit thought of the bloodthirsty tales being spread about the Tower ravens: how little these people knew!

'Thank you,' he said. 'I have not slept yet. In fact I'm not sure I want to.'

'But you are so tired, Kit,' said Muninn. 'You did not sleep last night either. We don't want you to be ill.'

'We can help,' said Huginn. 'Muninn and I can change your dreams.'

'They are Memory and Thought and birds like them have served gods in the past,' said Bran. 'They can show you visions of the past and future.'

Kit wasn't sure that he wanted to see either but something about having the ravens in his room, which had never happened before, made him feel so comforted that his eyelids began to droop.

'I am made of Memory,' said Muninn. 'But in dreams I can show memories of the past that didn't happen. That might have happened if events had turned out differently.'

She was speaking in a low clucking tone that soothed Kit right off to sleep.

And he was no longer in the Tower; he knew that straight away. He was in a very grand room in a palace – grander than the one in the Tower grounds. Kit was in a company of richly dressed and bejewelled people but he knew they could not see him: he was an observer of the scene.

At first he thought he didn't know anyone at this very grand party. But then he saw the queen.

She was younger and looking very beautiful in a gold brocade dress. She was dancing with a man with a red-gold beard and Kit realised with a start that it was a younger version of the king.

This must be from their courtship, he thought. *Muninn is showing me memories of when they were happy.*

But then a herald blew some notes on a trumpet and the musicians stopped while another couple entered the room. The man looked slightly familiar, with colouring like the king, and the woman was dark and though not pretty was lively and elegant. Both wore gold circlets in their hair. Three little boys dressed as for the court entered behind them, accompanied by their nursemaids.

Everyone shouted 'God save the king!', 'God save King Arthur!' and clapped, including the couple Kit had thought were King Henry and Queen Anne.

'What does it mean?' he asked in his dream.

What looked like a carving of a big bird on the panelling of the room stretched its wooden wings and flew down to him. No one seemed to notice.

'This is what might have happened if the king's older brother hadn't died. Arthur would have been king and Henry would have remained a prince. Arthur would have stayed married to Katherine of Aragon and Henry would have been free to marry the fascinating Anne Boleyn, even though she was not of royal birth.'

'And the king and queen had many princes?' asked

Kit. He craned to see Henry and Anne re-entering the dance as the music started again. They were both smiling, whirling around the room.

'They might have done,' said Muninn. 'Prince Arthur, Prince Edward and Prince Henry, perhaps . . .'

But the room was already turning dim, the dancers fading and the music dying away.

It was replaced by another scene.

It was a joust. King Henry, looking more like the present king than in the other vision, was about to enter the lists. It was a crowded scene but again Kit knew that he was invisible in it.

In the royal pavilion sat an older version of Katherine of Aragon, wearing a crown, and accompanied again by a troop of young princes and princesses. Kit recognised the Lady Mary, but she wasn't the eldest.

A black bird detached itself from the heraldic banner of a knight and came to rest on the wooden barrier between Kit and the lists.

'See the queen?' asked Muninn. 'Queen Katherine. The oldest prince is called Henry in this past. And there are more sons to ensure the succession.'

'Is Anne here too?' asked Kit.

'Look over where I fly to,' said Muninn. 'You will recognise someone else too.'

The raven flew to where other spectators sat and Kit saw again a younger Anne Boleyn, this time laughing and jesting with a young Thomas Wyatt. Beween them was a girl child that was certainly not Elizabeth, since she had black hair, and an older boy, who was asking his father lots of questions about the horses and their riders.

She could have been happy with him, or Henry Percy, thought Kit. *If only it had been like this.*

But he feasted his eyes on the picture of Anne laughing and holding her daughter until, as before, the scene faded.

He woke and found the room dark. Three ravens sat on the end of his bed.

'Sweet dreams, Kit?' asked Bran.

'No nightmares anyway,' said Kit. 'But still sad, because those things didn't happen, did they? Arthur *did* die and Henry and Katherine lost all their baby sons. Anne didn't marry her poet – if she had, she would still be alive.'

'But you see that what happens is only one of many possibilities,' said Bran. 'In another world those and many others might have been the pasts of Henry and Anne.'

'In another world?' asked Kit. If he hadn't been lying down already, he would have fallen. It had never occurred to him that there might be any other version of the reality he knew, that there might be other worlds in which the events of history unfolded differently.

'The same is true of the future,' said Huginn. 'Go back to sleep and I will show you something amazing.'

Kit lay back on his pillow, still exhausted and fearful but unable to resist the pull of sleep.

This time he was in a very different court. It was grand and full of exquisitely dressed courtiers but Kit didn't recognise any of the fashions, which seemed to him outlandish on both men and women.

This time Kit could see no one he recognised from his real life, as he glided among them listening to snippets of gossip. No Anne or Henry, no Katherine or Thomas Wyatt. He felt lonely and desolate, even though he knew it was a dream.

There was a lot of excited chatter as if the elaborately dressed courtiers were expecting someone. The doors at the far end of the Great Hall were thrown open and some even more gorgeously dressed women preceded into the room a queen that Kit had never seen.

She was neither young nor old and quite unlike anyone in Kit's experience. Her dress was stiff with gems – so many diamonds and pearls that it would have been difficult for her to sit down in it. Behind her head with its tower of burnished red curls a lace ruff stood stiffly up and her neck and hands were laden with more jewels. Kit had never seen anything more regal.

And a servant came behind her carrying a stand with a raven on it!

The big black bird had a ring round its ankle and a chain tethering it to another ring on the stand, which the servant placed carefully beside where the queen had come to a stop. She leaned over and stroked the tuft on the top of its head.

'My beautiful Bran,' she murmured.

Kit started. The raven was certainly like his Bran – a magnificent specimen. It started to caw and Kit could understand it. It was speaking not to the queen but to him.

'I am the descendant of your Bran,' he said. 'My grandfather was the chick you gave the queen that came from Blodwen's egg.'

'I never gave any queen a chick,' said Kit in Raven.

'I should have said that you will give,' said the raven. 'This is the future. And she wasn't queen then, only a young girl.'

His stand had a richly embroidered cloth with the golden initials 'E' and 'R' woven into it.

'Who is she?' whispered Kit.

'Why, it's Queen Elizabeth!' said the new Bran. 'The most glorious ruler the kingdom has ever had!'

Elizabeth! thought Kit. He looked at the resplendent queen and thought he could – just – trace a resemblance in her features to the little girl he had seen at Hunsdon.

'So she becomes queen after Henry?' he asked.

'Not quite,' said Bran. 'But she does become queen and that couldn't have happened if you hadn't saved her life.'

Kit felt his head spinning. Was this Bran or his descendant talking?

The musicians started to play a lively tune and the queen led off the dance with a handsome courtier, just as the scene began to fade again.

Kit sat up straight in his bed.

'Was that the real future?' he asked.

'As far as we know,' said Muninn.

'So the little princess will be queen one day? Her mother would be happy to know that.'

'And she doesn't forget you, Kit,' said Bran.

'But she was just a little girl and only saw me once,' said Kit.

'You are thinking of what happened a few days ago,' said Muninn. 'There are still many years to come before what you have just dreamed. The secretary will make sure that Lady Bryan brings up her charge to know the name of her rescuer.'

'And in time you will have a place at court, Kit,' said Bran. 'Elizabeth will reward you as her saviour. You will be her Raven Knight as you were her mother's.'

'So I *did* do some good?' asked Kit. 'I did save a queen. Just not the one I thought I was saving.'

After the Storm

ONE MONTH LATER

The poet was leaving the Tower.

Kit went to the bakery to fetch him some freshly baked rolls.

'You'll miss him,' said Isabel.

'I will,' said Kit. 'He has taught me a lot, especially in the last few weeks. I knew no poetry until he told me some of his.'

'I don't know any now,' said Isabel. 'You don't get much need for poems in a bakery.'

'That's where you are wrong,' said Kit. 'Thomas Wyatt has taught me that poetry is for every time and place. For sad times and happy times, for everyday use and for moments of danger and drama – like the times we lived through here a few weeks ago.'

'Will you read me some?' said Isabel.

'If you like,' said Kit.

*

Kit took the poet his washing water and his breakfast for the last time.

'I shall miss your visits and your conversation,' said Wyatt. 'Will you come and see me at my house?'

They were like two survivors of a flood or plague, different in age and rank but united by the experience they had lived through. Isabel and Alice were the same.

'If my father can spare me,' said Kit.

He hadn't quite returned to his normal self; he wasn't sure that he ever would. But the awful deadness that had overwhelmed him the day that the queen was killed had passed.

He went every day to stand by the slab in the aisle of the chapel under which the queen's body lay and said a prayer; he had promised to take the poet there as soon as he was released.

Everyone in the Tower lived as if they were cautiously picking up the débris after a monstrous storm had passed through, hurling off roof-tiles and demolishing walls.

Eleven days after Queen Anne had lost her head, the king had married Jane Seymour. Every trace of the Boleyn coat of arms was being obliterated from all the royal palaces and carpenters were again at work in the queen's lodgings at the Tower.

But for Kit and the others who had tried so hard to save Anne, her memory was not so easily erased.

The lord lieutenant came next door, to the Bell Tower, with his ceremonial keys, to release Thomas

Wyatt. His daughter came with him, curious to see a real poet.

'Ah, Mistress Alice,' said Wyatt. 'Kit has told me about you and I see he did not exaggerate your charms.'

Sir Edmund Walsingham looked at if he didn't approve of such flowery speech to his daughter. But then he took a closer look at Alice and saw that she really was a young woman and worthy of praise; it was a transformation that had happened while he wasn't paying attention.

The poet descended the stairs of the Bell Tower and took deep breaths of fresh air.

'It tastes of freedom,' he said.

Kit thought it smelt of the river, with all its wash of dead rats, rotting vegetation and salt from the sea. But he supposed even that was better than the stale air of a prison cell.

Wyatt shook hands with the lieutenant and took his leave. Alice and Kit went with him to the chapel so that he could say his last farewell to Queen Anne.

When they came out, they saw some ravens walking about in the grass between the recent graves, which were beginning to settle down.

'I wonder how long people will remember the men who lie there,' said Kit.

'You would be surprised, Kit,' said the biggest raven. It was Bran and only Kit could understand what he was saying. 'Kings and queens will come and go, but what happened here last month will still be written and read and talked about for hundreds of years,' said Bran.

'Really?' said Kit. He found it a consoling thought.

'But, Kit,' said Huginn, who was also there outside the chapel. 'The people of the future won't know what you did.'

'I don't mind,' said Kit. 'I don't want to be famous.'

'Who are you talking to?' asked Alice.

'Just the ravens,' said Kit. 'They told me no one will remember me.'

'And that makes you cheerful?' asked the poet. 'Most people want to be remembered.'

'Is that why you write poetry?' asked Alice.

'It is one of the reasons,' said Wyatt. 'Because life lasts such a very short time – sometimes much too short, as for the lady we have just prayed for. But words . . . well, some are snatched away on the breeze and live no longer than a stillborn babe. But some can outlive even walls as strong as the Tower's. We are still moved by the words of poets who lived over a thousand years ago.'

'Will you write about the men who lie here?' asked Kit. 'And the queen?'

'I have already started to, Kit,' said the poet. 'In my head. It will be a memorial that might last longer than a marble headstone.'

'It will,' said Huginn. 'You can tell him that, Kit. It might help him to get over his grief.'

So Kit told him what the raven had said and the poet stood a little straighter and taller as he walked out of the Court Gate of the Tower, ready to face what would happen next in his life.

'Well,' said Alice. 'It must be wonderful to be a poet.'

'But it's also good to be a Ravenmaster's boy,' said Kit. 'Come on – let's see if Isabel will give us a pastry. And some stale bread I can soak in blood for the birds. That's as much of the future as I can foresee today.'

HISTORICAL NOTE

Everybody knows the ancient stories about ravens at the Tower of London, don't they? That the city will fall if they ever desert their post? But when a man with the wonderful name of Boria Sax decided to investigate how far back these stories went, he could get no further than the nineteenth century. He wrote about it in his book *City of Ravens*.

The first big liberty I've taken with history is to make ravens a firmly established part of the Tower's life in the sixteenth century, with their own dedicated Ravenmaster. Thomas Wagstaffe and Kit, his boy, are my inventions. As is the adventure in which a queen is saved.

Thomas Cromwell was not present at the executions on 17 May but was in Hunsdon only in this book. Apart from that, I have been as faithful to the history of what happened in the months from January to May 1536 as I possibly could.

ACKNOWLEDGEMENTS

There really is a Ravenmaster now and the current one, Chris Skaife, has been very helpful to me, answering my questions and letting me visit him and the ravens.

Daniel Hahn kindly gave me a copy of his book on the Tower menagerie.

I wish Eric Ives were still alive so I could thank him for his wonderful biography of Anne Boleyn.

Hilary Mantel fortunately is still here to be thanked for 'strengthening my arm' with her perceptive comments.

CHARACTERS

Thomas Wagstaffe, the Ravenmaster

Marjorie, his wife

Kit, the boy they are raising as their own, who can speak Raven

Sir Edmund Walsingham, lieutenant of the Tower

Alice, his daughter

Sir William Kingston, constable of the Tower

Lady Mary Kingston, his wife

Isabel, the baker's daughter

George Atwood, the son of the keeper of lions and leopards

Ravens –

> **Bran,** the King Raven
>
> **Blodwen,** his mate
>
> **Huginn**
>
> **Muninn**
>
> **Thomas**
>
> **Bess**

King Henry the Eighth

Queen Anne, his wife (formerly Anne Boleyn)

Viscount Rochford (formerly George Boleyn), her brother

Jane Seymour, a lady in waiting

Sir Henry Norris, head of the king's privy chamber

Sir Francis Weston

Sir William Brereton

Mark Smeaton, a musician

Lady Mary, formerly Princess Mary, the king's daughter by his first wife, Katherine of Aragon

Princess Elizabeth, daughter of the king and the present queen

Thomas Wyatt, the poet, later Sir Thomas Wyatt

Sir Henry Percy, Earl of Northumberland

The Duke of Norfolk, Thomas Howard, the queen's uncle

The Duke of Suffolk, Charles Brandon, the king's close friend and former brother-in-law

Henry Fitzroy, the king's illegitimate son. He died of natural causes nine weeks after Anne Boleyn's execution, aged only sixteen.

An unidentified 'lord'

Thomas Cromwell, secretary to the king
Will Rede, one of his errand boys
Margaret Twynho, 'Mossy Meg', a witch
'Arthur Burford', a steward